REPERCUSSIONS

REPERCUSSIONS

ANTHONY SCHNEIDER

THE PERMANENT PRESS
Sag Harbor, NY 11963

FR

For information, address:
    The Permanent Press
    4170 Noyac Road
    Sag Harbor, NY 11963
    www.thepermanentpress.com

Library of Congress Cataloging-in-Publication Data

    Schneider, Anthony—
        Repercussions / Anthony Schneider.
        ISBN 978-1-57962-426-2
            pages ; cm
            1. Apartheid—South Africa—Fiction. 2. Political activists—
    South Africa—Fiction. 3. Exiles—South Africa—Fiction. 4. Family
    secrets—Fiction. 5. South Africans—New York (State)—New York—
    Fiction. I. Title.

    PR9369.4.S37R47 2016
    823'.92—dc23   2015042877

Printed in the United States of America

For Caro

1. SPEAR OF THE NATION

In the winter they started planting bombs. Nights were cold and the land was dry, and they blew up police stations and army buildings, pass offices and native magistrate courts, railway lines, pylons, bus depots. The idea was to create confusion and send a message, not to kill. *The time comes in the life of any nation where there remain only two choices: submit or fight.* It was time to fight.

Today the fight led Henry and his passenger down a mostly empty road that skirted the Vals River. They bumped along past low brick farmhouses, arid gardens, the tall spire of a Dutch Reformed church, drab fields. Mines glimmered in the distance, pockmarked slopes fringed by tawny scrub. Their destination, their target, was an army barrack near Kroonstad.

"Let's twist again," Henry warbled.

"Spanish Harlem," said his young passenger, whose name was Nxumalo, though everyone called him Orange. "With eyes as black as coal," he sang. "that look down in my so-oul."

"Crazy," Henry deadpanned. "For loving you."

Orange laughed. "Six Mabone. Sun Brothers."

THEY MET in suburban garages, safe houses, dark cellars. By turns cautious, brazen, philosophical, they debated which targets to bomb, planned attacks, considered resources, drew up checklists, restructured teams depending on who was in exile, on the run, at a training camp in Tanzania or Ethiopia, or in prison. They argued about why they were fighting and what each action might achieve. Nelson and Walter were the visionaries, Slovo and Mbede the warriors, Govan the conciliator, Rusty the planner, Bram the Afrikaner, Wolpe the lawyer. Henry and Dunningham were among the foot soldiers.

They spoke the language of ANC doctrine; the Freedom Charter was their mantra: a war to destroy apartheid, to win back the country for all her people. *Matla ke arona.* Power to the people. *Power to the sons and daughters of the soil, power to the oppressed and the poor.* They passed round banned copies of Marx, Engels, Fanon, Padmore, camouflaged in pilfered covers—*Little Women, Ivanhoe*. The High Command argued about Operation Mayibuye. Slovo pushed for war, Rusty and Walter for consensus. Of course civilian deaths were a tragedy, Slovo said, but they were unavoidable. They smoked cigarettes, drank tea and whiskey, confided in one another. They were all scared, but nobody talked about being scared.

Their homemade bombs were crafted from corner chemist supplies—carpet-cleaning products, chemical solvents, nitric acid, magnesium. Some of the bombs were equipped with rudimentary timers made of sea sand and glycerine, others with potassium chlorate fuses. They stole dynamite when they could, but it wasn't easy. Incendiary bombs required only petrol.

HENRY DROVE past the barracks and parked behind a field that abutted the compound. He switched off the engine and they sat there for a moment, then climbed out of the car without speaking. They proceeded on foot towards the row of squat brick buildings with red tin roofs. They walked under the cover of low trees, waited in a ditch across the road, watching to make sure no one was about. The idea was to get there before the new recruits arrived. His heart was pounding. His spine and back had tightened to the point of pain.

The compound was quiet, a few Bedford trucks parked outside, tarpaulins raised. Orange fastened the satchel across his chest, and they hopped the fence onto army property. He moved swiftly, torso bent, low to the ground. Henry took one last look at his watch, then followed, trying to run stealthily. Five minutes to get inside, ten to plant the bomb and get out. That would leave approximately ten minutes before the blast. He followed behind as Orange glided across the grass, well clear of the barracks and mess hall. They kept low, running around the perimeter of the property to the drill hall. Henry was aware of the sound of their footfall. They heard a car puttering along nearby, but there was no time to stop and look.

Henry was breathing hard when they reached the back door of the drill hall. A moment to catch their breath, then Orange opened the door. Inside it was dim—long tables, folding chairs, scuffed wooden floor. Orange pulled the paint tin from his satchel and set it down beside some chairs in the corner. Together they pried off the lid. Jack Hodgson, a British war veteran, was the bomb maker. His primitive timer consisted of a piece of cardboard taped over a small bottle of acid. When the bottle was turned over, the acid slowly seeped through the cardboard and dripped onto the powder, causing it to explode—and giving them only fifteen minutes to get out, sometimes less. Recently, the target had been a Johannesburg power station. Slovo, driving away, was nearly deafened by the explosion—just five minutes after he'd placed the bomb.

Henry pulled the bottle of acid from his pocket. He kneeled, carefully unscrewed the cap, and turned the bottle upside down on the sandy mixture inside the paint can. They held their breath. Exhaled when the moment passed without an explosion.

They opened the door slowly, looked for signs of movement, then scurried back to the edge of the property. They crouched behind a camphor tree before hopping the fence and dashing across the dry grass to the road. Glanced back at the mess hall as they scrambled back to the ditch. Waited. Leafless branches swayed in the breeze.

The explosion came suddenly, like a double thunderclap. Red glare in the blue sky. The smell of fire and burning wood, a hissing sound, dogs started barking. They stayed clear of the road, made their way through grass and bushes, and hurried back to the car.

As they drove away they heard the blare of fire trucks, dopplering away. Orange turned to look at the blaze. He seemed satisfied. Henry's stomach churned; he thought he might vomit. These were the front lines of the war for freedom. There was nothing elaborate or grand about it. They'd put lives in danger—their own, young soldiers', innocent black groundsmen's. They had destroyed property. And fled. You had to do your part. You had to trust the master plan. Later, when they told Joe and Rusty of their success, they'd cross the target off the list and congratulate Henry and Orange. And then, maybe then, he'd feel some pride, some sense of achievement. In the rearview mirror, he could still see the red glow on the horizon.

Joe Slovo and Abongz Mbede headed Umkhonto we Sizwe, the nascent military wing of the ANC. Spear of the Nation, MK for short. They had led many missions themselves. An army drill hall in Wentworth, a police station in Durban. Hodgson had turned his Hillbrow flat into a makeshift weapons factory, grinding permanganate of potash—used by restaurants to wash lettuce—into fine dust, and mixing it with aluminium powder. The mixture combusted when acid was added.

This was the winter of 1961. Henry and Sarah had moved into the house in Observatory. They'd hired a clown for Glenn's seventh birthday—*boerewors* and beer for the grown-ups, magic tricks for the kids. It was the year of *West Side Story* and *Spartacus*, the year South Africa withdrew from the Commonwealth, while all over Africa colonies were gaining independence. It was the year of JFK's inauguration and

Martin Luther King Jr.'s freedom rides. In the South African Parliament, the Nationalists increased their majority, while Progressives lost all but one seat. Walter Sisulu was sentenced to five-years' house arrest for not owning a reference book. It was also the year Henry had become a member of Umkhonto we Sizwe, the year he swore to bring down the government by any means necessary, to fight fire with fire.

So much had happened. The massacres at Sharpeville, Langa, and Mpondoland. Police had shot at unarmed crowds, killed women and children as they fled. Sixteen thousand were arrested for protesting the pass laws. A deranged white farmer had tried to assassinate Hendrik Frensch Verwoerd— aka the Prime Minister. The Unlawful Organisations Act declared both the ANC and PAC illegal, while an emergency decree gave the police sweeping powers.

Just a year before, Henry had been a garden-variety Communist sympathiser and outspoken critic of apartheid, like many people he and Sarah knew. But now he had gone further, first joining the Party, then the ANC. It was like growing up, taking responsibility. And it led here, to clandestine operations, to secret meetings, planting bombs and racing off into the night, waiting for the fear to subside.

Henry drove the borrowed car cautiously, careful not to speed. Orange held the map in his lap, the route carefully marked in pencil, but Henry didn't need to look at it. He knew how to get home.

They crossed the wagon-wheel Sarel Cilliers Bridge, passed chugging lorries.

"Why do they call you Orange?"

"It's a family name. When I was a baby, my auntie said my head looked like a big orange."

They drove beneath the darkening sky, under puffs of clouds and a big blemished moon.

"Where will you go?"

"Tonight? Back to Orlando. I'm staying with a friend."

"Go tomorrow," Henry said. "You can stay with us. Have some supper."

He could feel Orange looking at him, weighing up the offer. They'd bombed an army building together, but Orange wasn't sure about sleeping in a white man's house.

"We have to be careful," he said.

They would be, Henry assured him. He had to return the car anyway. They'd borrowed it for a night from a garage in Doornfontein. The owner, Yusuf Singh, provided cars, no questions asked, and relayed information. That was how the invisible army worked—a bit of borrowing, a makeshift network of sympathisers, a complex chain of communication, friends who helped and didn't ask questions. Sarah would have supper waiting when he got back anyway, Henry told Orange. They'd make up the bed in the study.

"I'll leave first thing in the morning."

Yusuf was waiting for them. He'd clean the car, make sure there were no suspicious marks, no evidence that it had been taken from the garage. They talked in the little office, surrounded by tyres, boxes of spark plugs and oil filters, exhaust gaskets. Yusuf had information about the day's activities. Bombs had exploded at power stations and government offices in Johannesburg, Cape Town, Durban, and East London. But at a police barrack in Johannesburg, Sam Dibakwane, dressed as a gardener and carrying a satchel, had to abort his mission when an officer stopped him. He smiled, Hello baas, and walked away, Hodgson's explosive sloshing around in a tennis ball can inside his satchel. In Soweto, their man wasn't so lucky. One of the bombs exploded prematurely at the Bantu Control Office. Lucas Bukhali was killed instantly. His accomplice survived but was badly burned, his left hand severed by the blast. Henry didn't know Lucas, but Orange did.

HOME. HENRY and Orange sat in the living room. Janey was in the kitchen getting supper ready. Having another black person in the house seemed to make her uneasy, upset the delicate balance—her employers' nod to equality of having her eat with them in the dining room. Or maybe she sensed what the two of them had just done, why Orange was there.

After a while, Henry went upstairs, washed, gave Glenn a good-night kiss, pulled the blanket over him. His boy was reading and writing now. Seven years old, and he could read the newspaper, was good at long division, could juggle a soccer ball. He built model planes in his bedroom, patiently gluing and painting the tiny pieces, drew elaborate pictures of houses with reticulated roofs and soaring turrets. Weekends they played soccer in the little garden or threw a cricket ball. Soon Glenn would be better at sports than Henry.

At the dinner table there was no ready conversation, and they ate cold chicken and drank red wine mostly in silence. Sarah asked politely where Orange came from. Natal. Did he have a wife? No. A smile. Just a boy, Henry thought, sixteen, eighteen at most. The face of a high-school prankster, not a terrorist. But he'd performed well, stayed calm. Henry wanted to say something. Here they were, two terrorists and two women, looking for all the world like some post-apartheid dream—two happy couples dining together. Only no one was happy. And they weren't two couples. One was a servant (who never drank with her employers), and two of them would be tried for treason and the destruction of government property if they were ever caught and linked with the crime they'd committed.

When they'd finished the meal, Sarah helped Janey with the plates. Orange sat at the dining-room table, oblivious or just exhausted. Henry stayed where he was as well. Bone-tired, now that the adrenaline rush had been replaced by the flush of red wine. You always wondered if someone had been killed by the bomb you planted. You rarely found out. You lived with maybe. Maybe people had died because of your actions. Maybe the attack would mean something. They sipped their wine and Henry stared at the night sky outside the window. *Come, seeling night.* Lucas, friend of Orange, was dead. Somewhere a mother was weeping. Could have been Orange or Henry. He had slept in a donga once. With Dunningham. He remembered the taste of dirt in his mouth, the cold night hardening around them. They'd planted a bomb outside the Sterkfontein police station. This was an act of retaliation, after the cops there had beaten an ANC man almost to death.

Henry hadn't been there to put his boy to bed tonight. Sometimes he didn't want to be read to, and Henry would lie beside him and they'd make up stories together. Glenn's tales involved soldiers and guns, daring cowboys, fistfights in saloons. Henry's stories took a more pacific bent. The cowboy who stole the moon, the horse who was afraid of flowers, singing mice, and treacherous banana peels. Weekends when the weather was warm they read in the garden— Henry, Sarah, and Glenn, each with a book and a cool drink, and sometimes Glenn would fall asleep curled up on the grass. Henry would watch him, his tranquil face, listen to his quick, even breathing. His boy. His son.

Henry and Orange finished the bottle of wine after Janey and Sarah had gone to bed. Orange said he'd head back to Natal in the morning. Henry wondered where he saw it all ending, whether he thought he could run forever, run into the future. They said good-night and clasped each other briefly at the threshold of the study, and Henry, slightly drunk and calmer now, felt a surge of emotion for this brave boy and comrade.

He climbed into bed beside Sarah and stroked her pale arm. She didn't turn around.

He smoothed her hair. "What?"

"Nothing."

"Come on. He had nowhere to go. What could I do, send him away?"

"Yes."

"Well, I don't think so."

She lifted herself for a moment, patted her pillow, and then curled back into the bed. Neither of them said anything, and the silence and the sound of the slapped pillow hung in the air. Henry pictured Orange downstairs in his unaccustomed bed. How good the freshly laundered sheets must feel to him, surrounded by walls of books.

Sarah reached over and touched Henry's face and neck. "Sleep now," she said.

But he couldn't sleep. He watched the branches swaying outside the window, inhaled her warm buttery scent. Was it just Orange's presence in the house, or was she angry about what he'd done, the whole enterprise? It was safer not to reveal details, not even to wives or husbands. But she knew, if not the details, then the type of mission. She probably thought he was going too far, but it was too late. He was one of them now. Umkhonto we Sizwe. Spear of the Nation. And they were going to change history.

WHEN SARAH came downstairs in the morning, Orange was already gone, the sheets and blanket neatly folded. She watched as Henry drank his coffee while Janey cooked scrambled eggs and tomatoes. Glenn told his father about a soccer match and somebody's birthday party. Henry was tired, fidgety; he didn't touch his eggs. Whenever Henry was late getting back, when he looked worried or went straight to the liquor cabinet, Sarah didn't ask, didn't say anything. What had he done last night? She didn't know the details, didn't want to know, but only one type of mission brought him home in the middle of the night with a stranger, smelling of *veld* and fire.

It was Mrs. Moore's week to drive the carpool, and Sarah waited with Glenn in the driveway until the white car appeared. And then Henry drove to work, leaving Sarah in the kitchen with a cup of tea, scanning the morning papers. There was no mention of an attack, but of course there wouldn't be.

A pamphlet distributed to newspapers and government offices later that day proclaimed: *The choice is not ours. We hope that we will bring the government and its supporters to their senses before it is too late.*

YEARS LATER, Henry would quote Malcolm X on the subject: "Concerning nonviolence, it is criminal to teach a man not to defend himself when he is the constant victim of brutal attacks." His grandson, Saul, would give him a baseball cap for his birthday with "Malcolm" stitched across the crown in white graffiti lettering surrounded by multicoloured Xs, and Henry would surprise everyone by wearing it and attracting strange though not disapproving looks on the streets of Park Slope, Brooklyn.

2. Woza Brooklyn

Henry, dressed in blue corduroys and old camel-hair coat, descended the stairs. He'd taken his lunch at the diner—a turkey sandwich and a Coke—returned home for a nap, and was now heading out for his late-afternoon walk, or crepuscular perambulation as he and Saul called it when the boy was still living at home. He was sure Holly, his daughter-in-law, was not home, but prepared himself for an encounter anyway, a bit of chitchat. Less privacy than when his home was his own, his castle. Still, there were meals now, his family around him, and the boy—until he left for college. Henry would have heard her on the phone, or the radio or TV would be on if she were downstairs. Nothing. Only the hum of the heating. He paused at the front door, pulled on his Malcolm X cap and cashmere-lined gloves.

Outside, the air was pleasantly cool. Winter's steely smell, patches of snow here and there on the sidewalk. The clear, bright days always reminded him of Johannesburg. Blue sky, the smell of grilled meat, the drone of a propeller plane would take him back. *Braaivleis, rugby, sonskyn en Chevrolet.* On the corner a kid in a beanie was skateboarding noisily, jumping on and off the kerb. A woman at the intersection laughed into her cell phone. Henry walking. He could go anywhere, do anything. Life—even somewhat circumscribed by age—was, if not glorious, achievable, still within his grasp.

Not that he didn't like his daughter-in-law. On the contrary, he loved her like a daughter, enjoyed her company.

The quick chats on his way out, or when she returned home, were always pleasant. He found he had more to say to her than to Glenn these days. Auburn curls, dark eyes coupled with a cheerful, unguarded expression. She bit her lower lip, had a penchant for floral patterns, drank only Irish breakfast tea. She had a sunny disposition, a smile like a truant schoolgirl and an easy laugh. Holly in her fleece and trainers, Holly with her healthy-living recipes. She made Glenn happy. A good mother, a good soul, a *gutte neshumah*. Worked part-time for Habitat for Humanity, volunteered at the local middle school. She had travelled to Ohio *sans* husband to campaign for Obama; she donated money to charities, took jury duty seriously. No, Henry had no complaints in the daughter-in-law department. Well, that wasn't exactly true either. Henry always had complaints. For instance, she could talk your ear off. About the most trivial things. One time, she'd followed him up and down the brownstone stairs, talking about the Barclays Center, and he made the mistake of suggesting that there wasn't much either of them could do about the construction of a basketball arena. Oy. Suddenly she went quiet, then proceeded to lecture him on the perils of not being part of one's community. She broadcast her opinions, was too loud about it all, talked too much, didn't listen properly, had little or no grasp of history or the rest of the world. Recently, Glenn had told him that Holly confessed to being a secret pot smoker. Never at home (Henry had never smelled dagga in the house). With some of her Habitat coworkers, apparently. They got stoned and went to movies on their days off. Once a month maybe. Nothing very wrong with that, Henry had said. "But she lied to me." Glenn was angry, wounded. Yes, Henry agreed, she could have said something. Why hadn't she? Would Glenn have said no, you can't do that? Henry didn't like to judge, didn't like to intervene. Other people's choices were their own. He stayed out of his son's life as far as possible. Still, he couldn't shake the feeling that he'd mucked things up.

He waited for the light to change, then crossed Eighth Avenue. The winter sky was a luminous blue above the frieze of trees, pale sun descending into the rooftops. The chimneys and water towers wobbled and warped, and Henry paused, squinting to bring them all back into focus.

In Prospect Park, he crossed the bike loop. A blur of bikers and skateboarders and rollerbladers whizzed past. He walked across the brittle grass past the dog run, under the swaying tupelos, their leafless branches hovering darkly. He was warm in his grey sweater and camel-hair coat and clumpy walking shoes—thick, ugly, old-man shoes. Sprouts of white hair under his cap, bushy eyebrows, his once olive skin now wan and wrinkled. But he was still handsome enough, he supposed, judging from the looks he got from widows and old queens. Henry sat on a bench, surveyed the scrubby meadow, the joggers and lovers. Sometimes when he walked through the park he remembered Zoo Lake in Johannesburg, the Luxembourg Gardens in Paris where he and Sarah had strolled on their honeymoon, even, somewhat hazily, Liverpool's Edge Lane Garden.

He watched the darkening sky, the trees, the mothers and nannies with their bundled-up toddlers, as the cold from the wooden bench seeped through his backside, chilling the bones. Not too cold to sit, though, to be outside in the world before dinner. He took walks more often, now that he lived in the city. In Stony Brook he'd walked to the beach sometimes, especially when they had the dog. Jupiter. But not very often, not every evening. The house, Long Island, teaching—that was all part of the past now. A little over four years ago, at Glenn and Holly's insistence, he'd moved from the Stony Brook home he'd inhabited for four decades to Brooklyn. He'd sold the house and given Glenn the bulk of the proceeds to buy the Brooklyn brownstone, which was big enough for Henry and Saul to have their own floor. He'd shared a bathroom with a teenager until Saul went off to college in the fall.

There were worse things, he supposed, than sharing a toilet with one's grandson.

When the sun was gone and the tops of the buildings looked like dark shapes cut out of the sky, he got up from his bench and walked home. The traffic was louder now, but he could still hear the wind in the trees, the faraway shrieks of children playing in the grass. He passed a young couple, hand in hand, a nanny pushing a double stroller, a family of Orthodox Jews. The fabled heterogeneity of New York—people in general—filled him with mild disdain. Trash on the park's meadows and lawns made Henry angry. People who smoked on other people's steps rankled him. Limos, Hummers, tourist buses, talk radio, the PA system in the subways, people who nattered incessantly on cell phones, newspaper circulars, unscooped poop, Dubya, takeout menus and locksmith cards tucked into doorjambs, disco, rap, reality TV, American chocolate, Slim Jims, green peppers, Jews for Jesus, crushed ice, Starbucks, the Weather Channel, Texas. Gah. He wasn't getting any friendlier with age, that was for sure. But he'd always been quick to anger. *I've told you. I don't eat tuna.* His son was calm but vaguely annoyed. *So don't eat it.* Wouldn't let it get to him. That's how Glenn was these days. Didn't suffer fools gladly, especially not his father or his son.

Sometimes, not very often, Henry got turned around if he didn't walk straight home or wandered deep inside the park. He hated asking strangers for directions, like a lost old loon. Half the time he couldn't hear what they were saying anyway. Black, white, Hispanic, everyone spoke like they had marbles in their mouths. And it wasn't just the way people spoke. Sometimes he could feel his brain flattening, fading, slipping, not only forgetting but also making connections that weren't there. He pictured a dusty machine in a wooden box, an intricacy of strings and pulleys, frayed and broken, bent and rusted. Cogs were losing traction. Words escaped him, failed to appear. What was that movie? So-and-so's husband? This, of course, had been happening for years, but it had been getting worse lately. Nowadays words sometimes came unbidden, language playing hide and seek. *Flannel. Vascular. Hibernian.* Some things were permanently stored, petrified in his mind. The beginning of the Lord's Prayer. A funny thing to be stuck forever in a Jew's memory. In two languages *nog*. Our father who art in heaven. *Onse vader wat in die hemel is.* Words he didn't know he knew startled him. He spoke them but didn't know what they meant, how he came to know them, even as they slipped out of his mouth, and the person he addressed—his grandson or a clerk in the grocery store— shot him an astonished look. *Tilsit, Ragnit, sand sock.* What the fuck, as Saul would have said. WTF, Gramps.

Homeward, the sidewalk awash in gathering shadows. Undulating grass, tall ash trees, aqueous light between the apartment blocks. The grand old buildings had surprised Henry—older, bigger than he'd imagined. All those years in Stony Brook, he'd barely been to Brooklyn, where so many Jews of his generation had spent their childhoods. Seventh Avenue. Frayed jeans and coats with elfin hoods, flip-flops in the winter, or boots like burlap sacks. What happened to proper shirts and shoes? Pants? A belt? Apparently it was cool to show the world your arse. Once in a while he considered saying something to one of them, but always stopped himself. Sarah wouldn't have approved. Or Holly. But Christ, what was next for them, underpants all day? Still, he liked to be among people, liked Saul's friends from school, most of them anyway, took pleasure in the human flux, the babble of the city, the hum of conversation, even if it wasn't directed at him and he couldn't always make out what people were saying. Yes, he liked the city, well, this slice of it, his family, the park, his newspaper in the morning and the sky at night. His room had a television set and an excellent mini audio system that Saul had installed and shown him how to use.

3. Nationwide

Nationwide Air from Johannesburg to Nelspruit on a shit-can flying bus. The overhead compartments rattled, the windows were mottled, the seat backs scored with assorted rips and cigarette burns. Flying time: forty minutes.

Kruger Mpumalanga Airport was small and new. They taxied past the single-storey control tower and walked across the tarmac to the arrivals lounge, which smelled of disinfectant and sweat. It was a lazy Tuesday afternoon, and the car rental attendants grudgingly roused themselves when the baggage carousel bell sounded. Saul found his rolling duffel bag and walked outside into bright light. He'd forgotten to pack sunglasses.

The taxi drove along the cracked tar motorway past dreary cement buildings, glass-fronted shops, a brick factory, a cluster of houses, then empty, lush land. The windows were open, and the air that flowed through the car was thick and hot. Below the drone of the motor he could hear birdsong and insects.

"You from overseas?" the driver asked, looking at Saul in the rearview.

"Yes. America."

He considered the answer for a moment. "Is it cold there?"

"Very cold. Winter. Snowing."

"*Haikona*. Overseas is very cold."

They passed a town called Hendrina, skirted Nelspruit proper, wove along the N40 towards White River. Billboards advertised Tastic Rice, Nokia, Suzuki Swift. *Rev up your night life.* They passed a herd of goats. The shepherd, a wiry boy, seven, maybe eight years old, watched them drive by. Abundant light, big sky, the smell of things ripe and growing. Bright sun on red soil, the land a thousand shades of green. A petrol station with a rusted red sign. It took him awhile to think of the word: beautiful. They turned onto a local road. Elephant grass, broad jackalberry trees, shadows, dust. Wild flowers leaned in the breeze. A tin-roofed general store, boys sitting in the shade, dark black and string thin. The land seemed to rise up, closing in on them, surrounding them, buzzing mightily. They passed *bakkies* and trucks, a rusted *Men Working* sign, though there was no evidence of anyone working.

The Leopard Mountain Lodge was north of Nelspruit, close to Bushman Rock and the southern end of the Kruger National Park. White buildings with thatched roofs. No leopards, not much of a mountain, but the rooms looked clean and comfortable and there was a pool. *Out of Africa* meets Pottery Barn. The nosey Austrian innkeeper, Mrs. Zöhrer, expressed interest in Saul's journey, professed that she loved New York, offered to read his horoscope or book a private plane to fly over the game reserve. He said no thank you, and asked if she would hire a driver to take him to Ka Nyamazane.

"But why do you want to go there?"

"I'm going to see a friend of a friend."

"From America?"

"Yes. A friend from university." He wasn't sure why he lied, but knew that he didn't want to go into the whole thing with Mrs. Z. Not now.

"It's not far," she said. "I've never been there, but my husband has. You can ask him if you like. There's a few locations like that around here. From the seventies. They moved people from Mbombela township."

"And you can hire a driver?"

"Yes, of course."

Saul nodded, thanked her, and backed out of the little reception area.

I<small>N HIS</small> room he put down his bags, checked the bathroom, turned on CNN, then switched if off again. He swam in the little pool. The only person he saw was a timid cleaning lady wiping the outdoor furniture. The sudden sun felt like a hot blanket as he climbed out of the pool. He lay on a chaise, breathing in the hot African air, smelling the chlorine on his skin. He could hear the hum of insects, the bush. Later he wandered the stone path that led away from the lodge, through dense vegetation, not venturing too far for fear of ticks or stray wildebeest. He passed two small birds with speckled bodies and red beaks, pecking around the edges of the road.

He ate dinner in the semienclosed dining room. A family was finishing their meal just as he sat down, and after they left he was the only patron. Wiener schnitzel, a glass of white wine, some sort of custard and canned fruit thing for dessert. Mrs. Zöhrer hovered briefly, inspected his schnitzel and told him she had contacted a driver who would phone or stop by the following day. He was back in his room watching CNN by nine, asleep by ten.

T<small>HE TRIP</small> was a gift from his grandfather. Thanksgiving, Saul had taken the train from his Ivy League turret back to Brooklyn, helped his mother make the gravy and sweet potatoes. After eating too much and listening to Henry rail against American football, grandfather and grandson had walked in Prospect Park. New York had turned cold very suddenly; their cheeks were pink and they could see their breath in front of them as they walked in the clear afternoon light.

"There's something I wanted to talk to you about," Henry said. "I'd like to suggest a Christmas trip. Go to South Africa. Get started on that documentary you keep talking about. Otherwise you'll spend winter break playing Wii tiddlywinks."

Saul had felt an old desire rising. For years, he'd been trying to learn more about his grandfather's past ("the bad old days" was Henry's phrase). Then he'd hit upon the idea of making a documentary, and although Henry rebuffed him when he requested an interview and snapped irritably when he inquired about old newspaper articles or asked if he could look through photos or books, Saul persisted.

"What do you think?" his documentary subject now asked.

"Great. You tell Mom and Dad?"

"They're thinking about it. I promised to foot the bill."

For Saul, South Africa was a place he'd visited a few times as a kid, mostly the beach; it was the stories his grandfather told, and the photographs in Henry's room. The photos were arranged on the bookshelf—a young man in grainy black-and-white with gleaming teeth, standing with his young bride under a jacaranda tree. Henry and the future president who did not become president, and, a few books along, Henry and the future president who did become president, in his trademark Madiba shirt, the two old men arm-in-arm, their hair more salt than pepper.

Resistance to Reconciliation was the working title. He would use newsreel, archival footage, and photos, as well as present-day interviews. He could interview his grandfather, Dunningham, Orange Nxumalo, other people Henry knew, maybe even Madiba himself. He had a video camera, would rent equipment, a crew, whatever else he needed once he was there. He had editing software, a friend at college to do the music. Winter break in sunny South Africa. Beach, sun, girls. Not having to volunteer at Habitat for Humanity with Mom. Hotel pools, bikinis, maybe a little tryst. Hey, you never know.

"There is one thing I would like you to do for me. I'd like you to look some people up. Old friends."

"Sure. Who?"

"Nellie and Ezekiel Mkhatshwa. Well, find them first."

"You don't know where they are?"

"They're not exactly on Facebook. My guess is they've left Johannesburg. Nobody I know is in touch with them anymore. I don't want to just let it go. If you ask around a bit I'm sure you'll find them. Might be interesting for you."

"Friends from the Struggle?"

"Yes, actually."

"That's cool."

Henry asked about college. Was there a girlfriend? A sore point. Granted, Saul was a bit pudgy, geeky, still had a few pimples. As his roommate cruelly put it, everyone else went to college to get laid—everyone except Saul.

Back home, his mother asked if they'd discussed the trip.

"Gramps mentioned it."

"And? What do you think, honey?"

"I think fuck, yeah."

"Language, darling."

"Sorry. Fuck, yes."

A MONTH later, Saul had taken the nineteen-hour flight to Johannesburg, checked in to the Westcliff Hotel, swum in the pool on his first day there. That evening he'd visited the home of Dick Dunningham and his wife, Daisy, Henry's old pals, whom Saul knew from childhood trips to South Africa. The taxi wound through the northern suburbs, under arches of jacarandas, past private streets and the walled exoskeletons of big houses. Razor wire, electrified fences, video surveillance, security company signs. Johannesburg had a locked-up, locked-in feeling. There was a sentry box and guard at the end of the Dunninghams' street.

Dick was a stooped, bald, suntanned, plump version of Gramps. For her part, Mrs. D wasn't a bit like Grams. Thin, pale, aloof, friendly but in a detached, somewhat formal way. They asked him about his grandfather, his parents, college, Obama. He told them about his idea of making a documentary. "I love a good doco," Daisy said amicably. "We can help you to get in touch with people, if you want. I don't imagine you'll be able to book Nelson, I'm afraid. But most of the others should be fine."

Could he interview Dick and Daisy? Of course. Did they have any old newsreel footage, home movies? No. The question seemed to astonish them. They sat at a table in a covered courtyard between the house and the pool, surrounded by white walls. A servant ferried plates of curried fish and salads. Moonbeams danced on the swimming pool; above the trees, the black sky was splashed with stars. Here he was, in Africa.

Dunningham knew Ezekiel and Nellie Mkhatshwa and confirmed that they were former comrades, but he didn't know their whereabouts. "Your grandfather was asking about them not too long ago." He did, however, know someone who might be able to find them: Hazel Simmons knew everyone from the old days.

In his cluttered, book-lined study, Dunningham thumbed through a worn leather address book and scribbled Hazel's phone number on a piece of paper.

"Anything you need, just let me know, okay?"

"Thank you. I will. Can I ask you something? Was my grandfather in the CIA?"

"No. Who told you that nonsense?"

"Some kid in college."

"Well, tell him it's rubbish."

"I did."

"No offence, but the CIA had a shit reputation here, still does, and your grandfather wouldn't have been caught dead talking to them, much less working for them."

Through the window he could see a dark lawn enclosed by a high security wall.

"How come they wouldn't let him come back? Like you?"

"Who says they wouldn't? He didn't want to. My children live in Australia and England. I've always envied Henry, having Glenn so nearby. And you."

"He says he did some bad things."

"I don't know. Necessary things. Not bad things. He's crazy about you, you know, talks about you all the time."

Saul left a message for Hazel the next morning. Waited for his phone to ring. It didn't. He drank two beers at the pool, watched the bikini-clad women as he ate a chicken sandwich. Back in his room, he masturbated vigorously, then napped.

The phone woke him. Hazel was chatty, with a smoker's rasp and an informal phone manner. Yes, of course she remembered Henry and Sarah—she'd known them very well, in fact. She had tracked Nellie Mkhatshwa to a rural township near Nelspruit called Ka Nyamazane. But there the trail went cold.

"No address, no phone."

"I could go there," he said.

"It's a far cry from Joburg. Out in the country. Don't expect too much if you do go."

He thanked her, and promised to send her regards to his grandfather, and she invited him to tea. Saul said he'd like that, thinking she might help him contact interviewees for his film.

He made one more call to book a flight to Nelspruit, and then went onto TripAdvisor.com to find a place to stay.

Dinner with Aunt Essie. They talked about Henry, and she reminisced a bit about Sarah. She didn't much like the idea of Saul going to a rural township. "Hire a driver. Don't try to drive yourself around in the middle of nowhere," she said.

"South Africa's a dangerous place." The next day he flew to Nelspruit in the old Boeing shitcan.

THE FIRST night at Leopard Mountain Lodge he slept well. He awoke to birdsong, bright light at the edges of the curtains, and the sound of someone raking the footpaths. It was almost ten when he entered the hotel lobby, and there was someone waiting near reception.

"Hey bra, how you, mate? I'm Sipho Nkosi. Your driver."

Sipho Nkosi, eighteen, maybe twenty years old, dressed like a fifties American gangster in an old leather jacket and fedora, even though it was summer outside, dusty wingtip shoes peeping from under his jeans. He walked with a limp. He pointed to the bad leg as they walked from the lobby to the lounge. "Accident last year, bra, hectic bad prang, but I'm fine." It emerged that, in addition to working as a driver, he was a small-time bookie. He smiled a lot, laughed a lot, and said everything as if it were the punch line of a joke. "You want to bet on Kaiser Chiefs, Bafana Bafana, talk to me, heh heh."

"Okay, definitely." Saul wasn't quite sure what to say to the chattering man.

"So, China, I hear you want to go to the location?"

"Yes, well I want to find someone who lives there."

"Where you from?"

"Brooklyn. New York City."

"Brooklyn. Jay-Z, Tupac, Denzel. Sharp. Do you have the address, phone number?"

"No, just a name."

"Okay. Just a name. I can ask some people."

4. A Meeting at Liliesleaf

Through the gate, along the wooded driveway, past the main house, Henry waved to the man in overalls, who looked like a gardener but was actually the guard. He parked next to the new T-shaped buildings at the back. He'd driven carefully, one eye on the rearview mirror, like a spy in an Edgar Wallace novel.

Increasingly, they'd been meeting here, at Liliesleaf, the sprawling house in Rivonia that the Party had bought the year before. Mandela had been the first political fugitive to make use of it, when, under the name David Motsamayi, he'd lived on the property. He'd worn simple blue overalls and played the part of a gardener. When black builders were working on the house, he'd made their tea, gone to the greengrocers for their sandwiches and snuff. Arthur Goldreich now lived there with his family. And in the servants' quarters and outbuildings, a steady stream of ANC members came and went.

An Indian man called Ravi sat smoking a cigarette on a bench made of cinder blocks and an old plank. Inside, Dunningham was talking to Slovo, Rusty, and Thomas Ngwenya. The room was mostly bare—cement walls, a naked bulb dangled overhead. They were waiting for Govan.

Joe Slovo was a garrulous man with thick wavy hair, big brown eyes, and a ready smile. Intelligent, warm, passionate, he was the one who pushed for armed struggle, argued with Nelson about how far Operation Mayibuye should go. Lately, he'd become more adept at sliding from rhetoric to sympathy, pugnacity to understanding, to get what he wanted. Slovo was a fighter, like Henry's Uncle Isaac. One who strikes back, hits hard, fights to the death. Henry admired them both. He and Joe had become fast friends. Henry, quieter, more aloof, recognised something in Joe, some dormant part of himself—the sense that he personally could bring about change. They had mutual friends, a shared background (Slovo was from Lithuania, born in Obelei, had arrived in Johannesburg when he was nine years old). Maybe Henry was unwittingly living out some childhood yearning—to help Uncle Isaac fight the war, to assist the oppressed, turn back the oppressor. But this was the Transvaal, not Lithuania. What felt familiar could in fact be lunacy.

Rusty was quieter, a pensive intellectual. Blond, blue-eyed and tall, he'd been orphaned at a young age, educated at Hilton College in Pietermaritzburg, fought in the desert war, and qualified as an architect. He listened, nodded, and gently moderated Slovo's plans. Rusty and Hilda lived with their four children on Regent Street in Observatory, near Henry and Sarah's new house.

When Govan Mbeki arrived, it was with Ezekiel Mkhatshwa, a young recruit, and his wife, Nellie. They talked about the previous week's missions. Henry got a hug from Mbeki. "Orange is a good chap?"

"Yes, very good."

"We give thanks to Lucas Bukhali and Sam Dibakwane," Rusty said. "Our thoughts are with their families." Not a prayer for fallen comrades, just thanks.

Mbeki introduced Ravi and explained why they were there. "We have a plan," he said. "A build-up of political pressure, culminating in a single day of sabotage across the country."

The plan called for coordinated attacks around the country on December 16, aka Blood River Day, aka Dingaan's Day, which was to be the official birth of Umkhonto we Sizwe. The dawning of a new era.

"Low-risk, high-profile targets," Rusty said. "Pass offices, native magistrates courts, railway lines at night. Bantu Affairs offices after business hours."

"That's easy," Nellie said. "In Jabulani, they always close early."

They all laughed, even Mbeki.

Nellie looked down, like a shy schoolgirl. She wore a green dress with a rounded collar and a thin blue scarf over her hair. It wasn't often that there was a woman among them.

They discussed details. Dunningham and Henry would do initial reconnaissance in Johannesburg, Zeke and Nellie would look for possible targets in Jabulani and Alexandra. Slovo and Mbeki would review their list and rank targets according to size and ease of access—no guards, no dogs.

Henry couldn't remember quite how it began—the stirring inside him fuelled by what he would later call the primacy of morality. The memory of his uncle roiling inside him, big Uncle Isaac who had left Liverpool to fight with the Vilna partisans. Perhaps resistance was Henry's birthright, in his blood, an innate belligerence. Henry, though mild-mannered and polite, was not one to avoid an argument or walk away from a fight—not since the Liverpool boys had beaten him up and stripped him of his Purim *hamantaschen*. Maybe that was the beginning—the seed, the tiny tree inside him. Also the grotesque injustice and inequality he saw around him, even as he was studying and then practising law.

Dick Dunningham, a friend from university—wealthy, urbane—had taken Henry to his first meeting. At a Wits' professor's house, they drank and talked in the living room, surrounded by crowded bookcases, the windows framing bougainvillea in a darkening sky. Fellow students, some professors, several members of the banned Communist Party. They talked about Cuba and an American group called Students for a Democratic Society. One of the professors said it was time to organise, to act. There was a growing movement to unite the mostly white Communist Party and the mostly black African National Congress. Henry felt a quiet elation at being there, listening to them talk about illicit actions and a cherished future, about change, a future free from apartheid. It was heady stuff, and he wanted in.

Dick had been Henry's first real friend at university. An unlikely pal—gregarious, family in England, a budding academic—he was studying literature and, with the help of his parents' gardener, teaching himself Zulu. They met in a sociology class and took an immediate liking to each other, talking about theories of sociology and how they applied to South Africa. They went for coffee afterwards, and to a Braamfontein bar a few days later. Dick asked about Lithuania and Liverpool, wanted to meet Henry's parents. That, Henry said, would have to wait. Dick dubbed him "The Velskoen Litvak" and invited him home for supper. The flat, which he shared with another student, was a big, messy place near Wellington Road, and there, most nights, they ate a communal meal, drank red wine, and discussed politics and literature until midnight. Henry drove home to his schoolboy room in his parents' house, drunk and happy.

Now, he listened as Mbeki talked about weapons, limpet mines, and AK-47s. There was money coming in, money to buy arms. They made another pot of tea. Slovo found a tin of rusks. As the meeting drew to a close, Slovo spoke to Ravi, Dick, and Henry. There was something else, another mission. He didn't have details. High priority and top secret. They were to clear their schedules on and around December 16.

The meeting adjourned, they said their good-byes, and Henry found Nellie's soft hand in his. He looked into her dark, gentle eyes as their hands touched, and then she was out the door with Zeke, waving good-bye.

Driving home, he looked at the swaying jacarandas, the houses with their long driveways, yellow light spilling from upstairs windows, and imagined bombs exploding, brick and steel and mortar riven, destroyed. Would it be enough? Would anything be enough?

HE KISSED Glenn, slipped out of his bedroom, then undressed in the dark and slid into bed beside Sarah.

"Late." She touched his face.

"A lot of things to plan."

"Be careful."

"I am."

She was up on one elbow now. "I worry. You guys are amateurs. You're not an army. And they are. They'll keep paying informers and making arrests. They won't stop."

"We won't stop either."

"School play tomorrow night. Don't be late."

They were careful. They limited contact with the network, didn't speak on the phone, watched for tails when they drove to friends or Liliesleaf. They'd learned not to trust the young soldiers who came from Angola or Natal unless a friend vouched for them. The police had moles and marionettes everywhere.

"Go back to sleep." He kissed her forehead.

But she stayed where she was, propped on one elbow, watching him with sleepy, serious eyes.

"We're a family now," she said. "You're a father. What if you go to jail?"

There had already been arrests. Men had fled, becoming exiles overnight. Others had been killed, running from police or fingered by informants and murdered. Some had been blown to bits when makeshift bombs exploded in their hands.

"You want Glenn to be orphaned, to be raised by my parents?" she persisted.

"Or my parents," he said curtly. She could be so melodramatic. A Jewish mama, all of a sudden.

"Or your parents. That's not the point. I need my husband here, in bed beside me, reading to his children at night, tucking them into bed."

There was no "them" yet, only Glenn.

Somebody had to say yes, I'm in, I'll do it. Peaceful demonstrations and letters to foreign governments weren't going to get the job done. Mandela quoted an old Xhosa proverb: *Sebatana ha se bokwe ka diatla.* The attacks of the wild beast cannot be averted with bare hands. And Henry couldn't turn around and walk away. Not now, not anymore. As Nelson said, "The methods we have applied so far are inadequate against a government whose only reply is savage attacks on an unarmed and defenceless people." He looked at you with those wise eyes, and you knew he was right.

"We're carrying the future on our shoulders," Henry told Sarah. "We're part of something hugely important."

"And your family, that isn't hugely important?"

It was all important. The meetings, the missions, the recruits, the training camps, the foreign visits, the foreign money, even the violence was necessary. There was a mountain to move; history would have to be nudged along. Henry had argued for uniting the Communist Party and the ANC. He remembered the war, little Lithuania like a piece of wood tossed about in a storm. The ANC and SACP needed each other, and as Sarah said, it wasn't as if Stalin really gave a damn about South Africa. Alliance was good. Fight power with cohesion.

They organised. They drafted memos. They got sympathetic letters from groups in America and London. But no action was taken. "We have to keep trying," Bram Fischer said. "No government is immune from foreign pressure." You couldn't argue with Bram. Somehow Afrikaners and blacks had the moral heft. It was their land, their people on the front lines; the Jewish liberals and the Indians in the Congress were all temporary sojourners – *uitlanders*. "Okay. We'll keep trying," Henry had said with a smile.

Meanwhile, people were dying. Thrown from police station windows, shot in the back at funerals and rallies. Every day brought more news of arbitrary arrests, men shackled together naked, beaten, a telephone directory held to their chests and punched repeatedly to avoid evidence of bruises and lesions, women raped, children orphaned. Meanwhile, the black majority lived in destitute squalor, still died of diseases like cholera, were regularly killed in random police raids. In Natal, a man called Philip Kgosana had recently killed a white farmer, shot him dead in his driveway. Henry wondered why it didn't happen more often—desperation's fury.

Compassionate, well-reasoned legal memos weren't enough. Prosecutions weren't enough. Protests weren't enough. The legal system was stacked against them. The Group Areas Act, Bantu Laws Amendment Act, the pass laws, the Immorality Act, the sabotage act. A growing body of lunatic laws made protest and free expression all but impossible. Movement was restricted, the townships locked down, rural blacks kept *op die plaas*.

Their efforts had crumbled, the petitions and memos and letters, like sand. And they needed rocks, not sand. Rocks and bombs, not legal briefs and pleading letters. Father Thorpe quoted Psalms: "Blessed be the Lord my rock, which teacheth my hands to war, and my fingers to fight." Once Henry started, it became easy to embrace violence, to work outrage into anger, feeling it grow deep inside him, a reservoir of rage and resolve. There simply wasn't enough time for legal proceedings, for talk, for other countries around the world to sit up and do something, or to wait for see-no-evil whites to take up arms. *By any means necessary*. That phrase again, picking its teeth with a bayonet.

He had decided, but Sarah wasn't sure. Even though it was she who had joined the women's march to the Union Buildings in 1956 and driven to and from Alexandra during the bus boycott the following year, ferrying people back and forth in the little Ford Anglia. But this was different; this was more dangerous. And of course, now there was Glenn.

SUMMER CAME to Johannesburg. Gardeners watered gardens; flowers bloomed, grass greened, and trees came into leaf. There were poolside braais and parties. The last weekend in November they left Glenn with Sarah's parents and went to Hermanus to see Henry's brother and his girlfriend. Mikey waited until dinner the first night to tell the news: they were getting married. Her name was Veronica, she wasn't Jewish, and she was pregnant. Veronica explained how they'd met— they were both nurses at the hospital. Mikey was saving up to put himself through medical school. They joked about Jewish doctors and Mikey in a nurse's uniform. They drank and laughed. The next day they all walked along the beach, watched the scurrying sandpipers, looked for whales but saw none, and ate at a French restaurant in town.

Back in Joburg, Henry helped plan a general strike and wrote pamphlets. *Awupatha. We shall not be dominated. Forward to freedom.* Sarah hired Rusty's firm to extend the living room and rebuild the servants' quarters, making the rooms bigger, modernising the kitchen that Janey and Ndimande shared, renovating the bathrooms and putting in new windows and heating, just like the main house.

The school holidays came, and Glenn was home all day. He watched the builders mix cement and plaster the walls, built model planes and balsa wood castles, and practised spin bowling against the garage wall. One Sunday after lunch he was running across the lawn behind the house and tripped. Face gobbled dirt. Wide-eyed and panic-stricken, he got up, looked around in surprise at the three grown-ups nearby, and as he began to wail, ran as fast as his little legs would carry him, to Janey.

SLOVO STOPPED by one evening unannounced. The plan for December 16 was coming together, and he wanted to make sure Henry wouldn't be away on holiday.

"No, not going anywhere."

"Good."

"What's the plan?"

"Something big," Slovo said. "A non-accidental, non-civilian death."

"A what?" And then: "You mean, kill someone?"

"I'll tell you when I know more."

5. SWIMMING

The beginning of his life was, to Henry, occluded, not remembered so much as imagined, pieced together from other people's memories and stories he heard. Loving mother, poor tradesman father, hills white with snow from October to April, the *shtetl*, Shadowa, not far from Vilnius. What he did remember was Liverpool. They'd left Lithuania when Henry was three, and subsisted in the port city while his father tried and failed to land a lucrative job. A year after they arrived in England, his mother's brother, Isaac, followed.

It was there, on a hot day in the summer of 1934, just after Henry's eighth birthday, that Isaac Dvoretsky knocked on the door of the narrow, woodwormy flat on the second floor of a stone building that rattled every time a car or horse-drawn cart rumbled past. Musty rooms with low ceilings, their dark wooden floorboards nicked and marred by thousands of boots and shoes; narrow windows hoary with snow and ice in the winter, and grimy in the summer months. In the kitchen a coal fire burned half the year, and it was in that kitchen, in front of the biggest window in the flat, that Eva spent most of her days, caring for Henry, cooking for her husband, or just sitting, allowing her body to nourish and warm the baby in preparation for its descent into the Liverpudlian cold and grime.

Isaac asked his sister if he could have Henry for the day. She was tired, worried about the rent as usual, and pleased, no doubt, that the boy would be out, helping with coal deliveries, as she believed. She made Isaac a cup of tea, apologising that there was no bread or cake.

Eva buttoned Henry's jacket and kissed him on the head. "Have him home before dark," she told her brother.

For nearly a year now, Henry had accompanied his uncle once a week, holding his big hand as they crossed the streets together and zigzagged their way down to the docks. The clatter of the tram behind them as they crossed Lime Street, Henry running to keep up.

Together they threaded through the narrow alleys around Saint James Street, the row houses rising steeply on either side of them, dark and solid beneath the pale sky. At the market on Penny Lane, Isaac sometimes haggled or traded all manner of items, from the whimsical—silk flowers or perfume for a lady; to the essential—shoes for Henry, a teapot for their mother. Sometimes he did deliver coal, but mostly he delivered food, blankets, and clothes.

And at the dockside, Henry would wait, kicking stones or watching the steamships at the landing stage while Isaac engaged in negotiations with sailors who spoke heavily accented English. Henry was always on the lookout for beer and lemonade bottles, which he sold back to the shopkeepers. He'd watch as his uncle opened little packages, chatting amiably with their bearers, nervous Litvaks and Poles just off the boat, and then give them an envelope or a tightly rolled wad of notes in return. Something about his manner seemed to reassure them, and the hunched immigrants always took their leave walking a little taller, faces more relaxed, after Isaac had shaken hands and clapped them on the shoulder.

Liverpool was dark and muck, cobblestones and stench; street vendors with handcarts; street urchins running in the alleys. In the company of his uncle, Henry traversed the city, rode the tram, saw men and women from all over the world—Germans and Danes, Frisians and Negroes, Jews from all corners of Eastern Europe, sailors and fish merchants, wealthy ladies with silk dresses, and barefoot orphans begging in the streets. Uncle Isaac even knew a Chinaman. He said that not all Chinamen were opium dealers. As it happened, this one was.

Liverpool was shipyards and soap factories, the smell of fish and bilge water and cold tenements buckled together, privies and ash pits and dank docks, men looking for work or not looking for work. Grey skies and tenebrous streets. Of course, there was sunlight on the sea and on the big ships with their soaring prows, and there was the stately Athenaeum Library that charged two guineas for admission, the Princes Road Synagogue and the tall cathedral off Hope Street. But mostly it was dark, the streets and tenements tangled and grey.

Henry. Shock of brown hair, green roaming eyes, small and lean, in a coat many sizes too big. He didn't go to school, the only boys near Captain Wilson's building where his family lived were older. When he appeared carrying a box or bag of groceries or goods from Hibbert's, they taunted him and threatened to rob him, and sometimes they did. Uncle Isaac was his constant companion. It was Isaac who told him about Big Jack Johnson, heavyweight champion of the world, and Harry Houdini, who could escape locks and chains, the Wright brothers who built a flying machine in Kitty Hawk, America, and Amelia Earhart who flew across the Atlantic. Henry dreamed of boxing, magic, of flying across the wide blue sky, or, like Harry Houdini, escaping.

Uncle Isaac. Six feet tall, thuggish and sweet, woolly beard, soft green eyes. A seafarer's face, though he'd never worked on a ship. Isaac, whom Henry's mother called Itzchak. At the end of a day spent at the docks, or wandering in and out of taverns, or making deliveries to scattered locations, they would dart into a lane and find a coal hatch where they blackened their hands and clothes, with a dab on the face or neck, before Isaac returned his charge to his sister. If it had been a good day, Isaac might sing as they walked home, sometimes a sailor's tune, but more often a snippet of an aria or symphony, a wordless *Ya de ya da dem*, his head bobbing, sooty hands rising in the air to conduct an invisible orchestra.

Once, Henry asked his uncle what he was singing, and Isaac replied, "Bach, beautiful music, boychik." And taught him a passage, and they sang it together, louder and louder, walking down Rathbone Street, puffing tiny clouds in front of them, like little ghosts dancing and collapsing in the cold air. The next time he visited, Isaac brought his violin, let the boy press and pluck the strings, tap the bow and run it across the strings and make high-pitched screeches, which Isaac applauded. Small, pale Henry held the instrument under his neck the way he'd seen Isaac imitate violinists. For even though his Great-Uncle Zalman had been a celebrated musician, Henry had never actually seen anyone play the violin. "Here, Henry, you draw the bow across the strings," his mother urged. The next attempt was, if not music, certainly a more bearable screech. "You'll be a great violinist one day," Isaac promised. He left the instrument with them, and Henry occasionally produced a sonorous note.

He sometimes played for his mother in the afternoons, just the first bars of a Bach adagio, stretching the notes, pulling the bow until the sound warbled and faded, then bowing the next note, the fingers of his left hand moving slowly, steadily, feeling the shape of the music on the violin's neck. When they put on a gramophone record he would often play along, picking out a few notes of the melody and repeating them. He was no Zalman, but the accompaniments he played were, in their own way, soothing and stirring in their slow methodicalness. He didn't hit many wrong notes or make the instrument screech any more.

That hot summer day in 1934, Henry's father, who had owned a leather shop in Lithuania, was working on the docks, unloading crates for a shilling a day. It was a matter of time before he'd quit, or get fired, and then drink and grumble for a few weeks before finding another job. He was impatient and inventive, having made his way in Shadowa by being the first to learn what styles were in vogue in Saint Peters-burg and Paris and engaging a seamstress to copy them—elbow-length flapper gloves for the ladies, thick stitching with plaid lining for the men. Nor was he above sewing a French label on the inside of the wrist. Duluc. French gloves, *alevai*. And now here he was in Liverpool, doing manual labour. Jakub was not a big man, and despite having strong leather-workers' hands, the work tired him and made his back ache so that he couldn't sleep at night. Then he would shout, at his wife, his son, anyone within earshot, and go drinking with the other Litvak *shlemazels*.

After waving good-bye to Eva, Isaac and Henry picked their way down Cecil Road, walked past the Sailors' Home and along Pitt Street, past the Clarence, and boarded the bus to Bootle, disembarking in the midmorning sun. They crossed the busy high street, away from town, seeking the shade of trees as they walked. They passed rows of new houses, emerg-ing at last on a grassy bank of the Leeds and Liverpool Canal, near a bridge. There was no one about. Moss and lichen on the stones; a ripe, rotty smell rose from the brown water.

Isaac folded his jacket and lay it down under an oak tree, then slowly undressed until he stood in his undershirt and drawers. Henry copied his uncle, standing in the shade. Slimy grass and rocks slippery and warm bordered the water into which they carefully stepped until it covered their feet, then their ankles, and then it was above Henry's knees, warm mud sliding between his toes. Isaac took his hand and led him along the muddy path to the spot where the embankment rose to its highest point above the canal.

"Come on," Isaac called, and Henry felt his hand let go and watched his uncle dive into the water, felt the splash. The water coiled and rippled, and then Isaac was up above the surface, his dark hair wet and shiny, his white undershirt gleaming.

Henry watched from his perch on the mossy bricks, muscles twitching, then reached forward and lunged, landing belly first in the water, eyes closed, legs pumping. He didn't stop thrashing until he felt Isaac's big hands surround him, hoisting him up. The water was cool, and the sun made diamonds of light on their water-speckled chests and in their eyelashes.

The next dive was easier, the water did not sting so much, and the time after that was more fun than scary. "Like French aristocrats on the Riviera," Isaac said. "Come on, watch me." And he would dive gracefully into the canal, surfacing some distance away. "Come on, Hen. Arms out in front of you, now fly."

Soon they were diving in side by side, arcing into the sunlit canal, aloft together in a silent floating moment, then drawn down into the water. When they surfaced a few seconds later, spitting out twin plumes of water and laughing, Isaac exclaimed, "You're a natural, boychik."

THERE WAS a heat wave that summer, and twice they rode the train to Southport, taking a bus from there to the beach at Ainsdale. They walked the crowded esplanade, past women under broad parasols and men in striped shirts and plimsolls. Henry could smell not just docks but the sea—salt and brine and magnitude. They stripped down to their baggy drawers and ran into the water. Cold waves crashed loudly, and together they jumped in and out of the salty surf.

Wherever they swam, wherever they travelled, on the way home they always stopped at the grocer's on Richmond Road. Milk and a Nestlé bar for Henry, tobacco and a bottle of Threlfalls Blue Label for Isaac, as well as a loaf of bread, lamp oil, sweets, and soap for Henry to take home. They would sit on the steps, and Henry would drink his milk and eat his chocolate and feel his uncle's smiling eyes on him, and the warm stirring inside him was something he would later come to call happiness.

6. Park Slope

The house was quiet. The rumble of the ice maker, like something prowling. A toilet hissed. Holly was probably at work, or out shopping. He could never remember her schedule, even when she posted it on the fridge under a magnet that looked like a piece of sushi. A dusty, unappetising piece of sushi. A year ago, Saul would have been home from school by now. Henry missed the boy, their afternoon chats, playing chess, walking to the shops or park when Saul should have been doing homework. He took too long in the bathroom in the morning, and they bickered whenever Henry tried to help with schoolwork, but they'd made their peace, learned to coexist happily. Now there was one more person pulled from his life, one more person for Henry to miss.

GLENN ARRIVED home first. He hung up his coat, stuffing a striped scarf inside the arm. Standing in the doorway in his grey suit and grey shirt, he looked tired. Crow's-feet at the edges of his glasses, dark rings under his eyes. A bit more rumpled and pudgy than the cool architect of a few years ago.

"Turn on some lights, Papa."

Henry rose, and followed him into the kitchen.

"Must have dozed off. How was work?"

Glenn stood at the marble counter, opened the fridge, surveyed the contents for a moment, then closed it. He poured himself a glass of water from the Brita filter, and drank it staring at the sink.

"All right. Busy and barely profitable. Story of my life."

"The renovation going okay?"

"Yeah, I guess."

That was Glenn. Laconic. Henry didn't know much about his son's current projects. His firm had completed the design of a restaurant for a Disney cruise ship, but there was no more work coming from the land of Mickey Mouse. They were working on a townhouse on the Upper East Side and a three-bedroom apartment renovation—not the type of projects they'd have taken on a few years ago, but you didn't turn work away these days.

The mortgage crisis had been doubly cruel to them. Glenn's practice had suffered, and their best-laid real estate plans, a building in Red Hook, had gone belly-up. But if Henry had erred, it had been out of love, out of confidence in a financial market that everyone had trusted, not a market that plummeted, leaving banks reeling with toxic debt. They had their own piece of toxicity now. He couldn't begin to tell his son how differently he'd imagined things, how much more he'd wanted, not from Glenn, but from himself. Their investment was underwater. The expression chafed him. New Orleans, now *that* had been underwater. Atlantis. But this was New York City. He felt betrayed—and poor. All his life he'd made good investments. But not this time, boyo. He'd aimed, if not for wealth, then for financial security. Had he messed it all up, after all these years? It appeared he had.

Henry switched on the kettle. They'd drink a cup of tea and talk. Henry liked to have things out, to talk until they'd found the nub, whatever it was. Except with his son. Where did this reticence come from? Born of old resentments? A family trait (on his mother's side, of course)? Whatever its origin, their modes of communication were too diverse.

"See Holly today?" Glenn asked.

"No."

"I wonder if we should order something. I'll call her and ask."

Glenn never complained about Holly's schedule or non-profit jobs, never suggested that she try to earn more or look for a better job.

"Have you talked to her?" Henry asked.

"About?" Glenn glanced at his iPhone then stowed it in its cradle.

"About the dagga." He found it hard not to smile at the image of Holly, feet up, smoking a bong.

"Pot, Dad. We call it pot."

"Whatever." Another expression he'd picked up from Saul. Poor Glenn. Holly had her escape—her friends and illicit drugs. All Glenn had was work. Maybe all sons bewilder their fathers, Henry thought, looking at his boy, a harried middle-aged man—and remembered little Glenn crying because his nappy was wet.

"You know, the other day," Glenn said, looking at the kettle, "I was in the kitchen and there was white powder on the counter. I was ready to march in and accuse her."

"Of course."

"I tasted it. Put a finger in the powder and tried it. Flour. She'd been adding flour to the stew."

Henry wished it were easier to talk, freely, like pals. "Flour. Funny," he offered.

"Yeah, well. But, you know, I just don't trust her anymore."

"She smokes a bit of pot. Can't you live with that?"

"Or course I can. But it's a breach of trust."

His son was in the throes of Kierkegaardian despair. A despair that is unaware of being despair. Kierkegaard, despair, depression: these were things he couldn't talk about with Glenn.

"I got an e-mail from Dunningham," Henry said. "He thinks Saul is a fine young man."

"Good, so he's behaving himself. Not being a brat."

"He's not a brat."

"He can be. You know that."

"Sure. He's a twenty-year-old."

"Well, do all twenty-year-olds sulk and complain all the time? He told Holly she was boring, to her face. I mean, I can do without the attitude."

It was true. Saul could be mildly contemptuous of anything and anyone, especially Glenn, who generally bore his son's scorn with quiet stoicism. Once in a while, though, he cracked. Like the time Saul had made fun of his hemorrhoids; that was the latest blow-up. "Go upstairs," Glenn hissed through gritted teeth. "Get out of my sight." But for the most part, he seemed more surprised than angered by his son's behaviour, never having gone through his own revolt—too uncertain of himself after their arrival in America to risk pissing Henry off. It took a secure kid to make fun of his dad, but there was no telling Glenn that. After Saul went to college, it got worse. Glenn would talk about movies or plays he liked; Saul would call them bourgeois or predictable, dismissing a movie with a flourish: "That's a pretty hackneyed meta-narrative, don't you think?" End of conversation. Poor Glenn. Kierkegaardian despair, estrangement from his only son, and Preparation H. He deserved better.

Henry watched Glenn put a teabag into each of their mugs. He looked sad and tired. His son. His boy.

THE FRONT door opened with a gust of cold air and the crackle of grocery bags. Holly in bright colours, cheeks pink with cold, her auburn curls tucked under a candy-striped hat. A kiss on the cheek for Glenn, a kiss on the head for Henry, then she padded upstairs to change, appearing a few minutes later in a purple fleece and sheepskin slippers.

Holly cooked; Glenn made the salad; Henry laid the table.

Dinner wasn't the same without the boy. Holly's lamb chops and Glenn's healthy salad, which Henry knew not to criticise. As Saul had done at so many meals, he knew to move the salad around on his plate. Henry missed the boy's sporadic dinner chat, a word or two at best in response to any question designed to coax some conversation from him, and then a sudden babble—about a movie, a Tweet, his friends. Without the boy around, tonight's questions were directed at Henry.

"Papa, did you make the appointment?" Glenn asked.

"Slipped my mind."

"Maybe you can do it tomorrow?" Holly suggested.

"I've seen the doctor. He's my doctor."

"But we also want to see him, okay?" Glenn said. "It's for us, not just for you."

First Nat Cusson and then the other one—Sieve, Sliver, Silver, the neurologist. They were his doctors, and Glenn went rushing from one to the other without even the courtesy of telling him, let alone asking. He knew what they hadn't told Glenn about: his visual agnosia. He saw things but couldn't always tell what they were. The world sometimes separated into abstract forms, a watery scrim of rippled shapes, splotches, and wriggling colours, and he had to concentrate very hard and wait a few seconds for it all to cohere again. His retinas were undamaged, but the neural pathways got confused, sending the wrong message to the brain. They'd done an ultrasound, a CT, and a SPECT scan. A ministroke may have caused the neurological damage, or maybe it was mild dementia, or early-stage Alzheimer's, which would account for the mental lapses, the unbidden words. The doctors smiled when they'd told him this. They recommended PET scans and talked about plaque and tangles. They all had big white teeth. But they wouldn't share his records or divulge his diagnosis with Glenn. Not without Henry's permission. Patient-privacy protection. God bless America.

7. Ka Nyamazane

Thursday morning. Sipho was waiting in the lobby again, dressed in a brown shirt, jeans, and the same wingtip shoes.

"I found Lillian Mkhatshwa for you, bra," he said triumphantly. "That's Nellie's daughter or maybe her granddaughter." He raised his eyebrows as if he'd arranged for Saul to go on a date with Miss Mpumalanga.

"Cool."

"Ja, cool. Brooklyn style. I'll phone her."

Sipho smiled as he chatted on the phone. Saul sensed that the person on the other end of the line was neither as excited nor as loquacious as Sipho.

He handed the phone to Saul.

After some bumbling explanation, Saul got across the idea that he would like to pay a visit. Perhaps she knew his grandfather?

"Henry? Yes, yes, of course," Lillian said. "You're his grandson from America?"

"That's right. Could we come today?"

"Okay, today. That guy, Sipho, he knows how to find us. Modisana Road in Ka Nyamazane."

Saul went back to his room for his camera, phone, and backpack. When he returned, Sipho was leaning on the side of a battered Toyota Corolla, the colour of pea soup.

They shook hands again for no apparent reason. Maybe that was Brooklyn style. Then they negotiated. Sipho charged what seemed like a reasonable amount compared to, say, the price of a hotel room, and made Saul promise to buy lots of beer for the trip. Saul wondered if he should tell his mother he was getting a lift to a rural township with a drunk who'd been in a bad accident only months before. Maybe not.

It wasn't yet noon when they pulled off for petrol; Sipho downed two Black Labels before they got on the highway again. They wound along, around a mountain, then onto a rural road—dusty tar, grey, and splotchy. Sipho drove fast, and they sped past bushy slopes, acacia trees blooming in bright patches. Glancing at his passenger, Sipho explained that he also worked as a tour guide, bought and sold tickets to sports events, and took bets on rugby, soccer, and horse racing. The car kicked up dust as it sped along, and the land buzzed around them, the trees throwing shadows on the road, while undulations of bush and sky quivered in the rearview mirror.

The road gradually grew narrower and more uneven. The car bounced along, scraping rocks from time to time. In the middle distance, a few flimsy shacks hunkered between trees.

"Yebo, Saul. Ka Nyamazane. That means the place of the animals. Lots of, how do you say, animals like kudu?"

"Buck?" Saul said. Thinking: kudu, voodoo, Urdu.

"Yebo, buck. You know there's not so many lions anymore. Everyone always asks, show me the lions, man. I say I can't, bra. The lions they are dying. They got like HIV. Bad stuff if you are a lion, hey."

The windows were open; hot air tumbled through the car. Saul knew better than to ask about air-conditioning. They sped through flat grassy *veld*, punctuated by the odd lonely *koppie* rising into the wide blue sky. The car rattled and squeaked. They left a trail of dust in their wake.

And then the open land gave way to buildings again. It came upon them suddenly, the mishmash of houses and humanity, small, low shacks, jumbled and haphazard beneath the sky, on the slopes of a mountain. Shirtless children played at the edge of the road. Men sat in the shade on dilapidated chairs and milk crates. Some of the structures looked half-built or looted, it was difficult to tell. Smoke curled into the sky, and the wind carried the smell of cooking and human habitation. The rutted road, more houses, all more or less the same, cinder block and corrugated iron, all with barred windows and locks. Some had brightly painted doors, orange or blue; others were protected by suburban security gates. He noticed a couple of little houses made of stone and rough cement. To their right, more shacks sloped towards a ravine. On the other side of the road, another phalanx of houses threaded with paths beneath the looming mountain, fuzzy with foliage.

They parked in a narrow driveway on Modisana Road. Here the houses were larger, made of brick, with sloping corrugated iron roofs, glass windows, and white-painted burglar bars. There were no cars parked outside the houses.

Sipho climbed out and walked towards the house. Saul followed, his head spinning a little as he stood up in the heat.

Cinder block columns supported a small canopy over the front door. On the small cement *stoep* painted dark red with hairline cracks here and there, stood three wooden chairs and an office chair no longer on its wheels. Behind a black metal gate, the front door itself was painted royal blue and bore the house number painted by hand: 932.

Sipho knocked on the door. The woman who answered—Saul's age, maybe a few years older—smiled at Saul as Sipho spoke quickly, suddenly rather formal, hat in hand.

There was another voice from within, small and high-pitched, and then a little girl appeared behind the woman; three, maybe four years old, she peeked around her mother's legs at Saul.

"This is Lillian, man," Sipho said, then kneeled down and cooed at the little girl in the doorway.

"You're Lillian Mkhatshwa?" Saul ventured.

"Yes. And this is Dimpho, my daughter. Say hello, Dimpho."
But the little girl scampered off. Lillian held out her arm, and
they shook hands.

"Good to meet you," Saul said.

She was slim, with a long face, high cheekbones, and
skin that bore the purplish scars of teenage acne. She wore
an orange-and-blue scarf around her head.

"I've heard a lot . . . well, I haven't really heard anything
about you," Saul started off stammering, then took a breath
and tried to speak more calmly. "But I've been wanting to
meet you. I was expecting someone a bit older. I thought you
and your husband may have known my grandfather."

The child emerged again, cautiously, gripped her mother's hand and studied Saul.

"Please come in," Lillian said. "But we haven't got anything much to offer you." Then she turned to Sipho and they
conferred in Zulu.

"She wants to go to the shops."

She'd obviously said much more than that, but Sipho had
chosen to summarise.

"Sure. Great."

Lillian locked the front door, and they all climbed into
Sipho's car, Lillian and Dimpho in the back, and started down
the rutted road.

"Have you ever been here before?" Lillian asked.

"Here? Never. Only Johannesburg—and the beaches."

They parked at Mbebe Centre, about two kilometres
away. Location shopping mall. A two-storey building flanked
by shops with barred windows and wooden kiosks sheathed
in blue tarpaulins with hand-painted signs. *Veg/Fruit, Telkom
phonecards, Liquor Beer*. It looked, Saul thought, like a bad LA
neighborhood after the apocalypse. A Castle Lager billboard
towered above the rickety outdoor stalls. Men and women
carrying heavy shopping bags walked by; others sat in the
shade. Sounds of conversation and laughter, grumble of traffic, tarps flapping in the wind. A brassy disco song played

somewhere in the distance. The walls of Tango City Barbershop were adorned with handsome torsos sporting sunglasses and fade haircuts. They passed a phone and Internet café, Jackie's Beauty Salon, a butcher shop. A group of girls—eleven, maybe twelve years old—in sneakers and bright sandals. Farther down the road was Sumba's Auto Repair, Levisa Fried Chicken, and the HR Lounge, its turquoise and red sign askew above the door.

Dimpho ran ahead. She wore cut-off jeans a few sizes too big, pink-and-white sneakers, and a T-shirt emblazoned with fading stars and donkeys. She stopped at one of the shops and waited.

Ten City Grocer was dim inside, its shelves partially empty. An old man in brown slippers and frayed khaki pants sat on a barstool beside a cracked glass counter. He smiled and said hello to Lillian. Saul scanned the shelves. Cooking oil, potato chips, condensed milk, tinned peas, carrots, sardines, toothpaste, light bulbs, toilet paper. Closer to the counter where the old man sat, there were loaves of bread wrapped in paper and a battery display case. Behind the counter the shelves were piled with snuff, shampoo, cigarettes, aspirin.

They bought Cokes, fruit punch, milk, a packet of cookies, and a six-pack of beer. Saul paid. Everything except the milk was warm.

On the way back to the house they chatted stiffly. When Lillian asked where he was staying, Saul gave the name of the lodge and Sipho added some explanation in Zulu. She looked impressed, and Saul understood that here he was regarded as rich.

Back at the house, Lillian unlocked the gate, and they carried the groceries inside. Saul found himself in a small living room. The house design was simple, two interlocking squares, the larger one comprising two bedrooms, living room, and bathroom, while the smaller square housed the kitchen and water tank. The kitchen, bathroom, and living room floors were tiled in white.

Following Lillian to the kitchen, Saul glimpsed a small bedroom containing a single bed. The cement floor was covered with a rug, and small reproductions of flower paintings hung on the walls. A larger bedroom was less tidy. The dressing table was crowded with an array of cosmetics. Lillian's room, he presumed.

The kitchen was narrow, with a sink and metal counter. There was a cistern above the sink, with a plastic water drum beside it. Lillian opened the back door, affording a view of twin sagging lines that held no washing, only a few clothes pegs like sclerotic birds on a wire. Down the way was a small brick house with a tin roof. Above its back door a sheep's skull presided eyeless over the tangle of trees and shrubs.

"Can we help with anything?" Saul asked.

"Thanks, but there's nothing to do," Lillian said. "Have a drink in the meantime. Relax."

She handed Saul a Coke and gave Sipho a warm beer. Dimpho exclaimed happily.

Saul wandered back inside the living room. Against the length of a wall stood a peach-coloured wooden sideboard. On top of the sideboard sat a bowl, a stack of blue-and-yellow place mats with curled-up edges, a large black radio, unplugged fax machine, and a row of framed photographs. Inside the sideboard were books, two photograph albums, a Bible, teacups and saucers, and a stack of magazines. There was a dining table with five chairs, and near the front door, a brown couch and two old armchairs flanked a wooden coffee table with intricately carved legs.

He walked outside, where he sat beside Sipho on old chairs in the shade. Sipho had finished half his beer when they heard the door squeak open and Lillian and Dimpho appeared. Dimpho walked with great care, carrying a plate of cookies, and they each took one.

"*Ngiyabonga*," Saul said in his best Zulu accent, and Dimpho giggled.

"This house belonged to my grandmother Nellie," Lillian said, sitting beside them. "The one who knew your *umkhulu.*"

"And where is she now, Nellie, I mean?"

"She passed. One year ago."

"I'm sorry."

"Almost exactly one year." She looked up at him but offered nothing further.

The words hung in the air, and no one said anything for a moment.

"And Ezekiel?"

"We don't really know too much about him. Your grandfather knew him as well, I'm sure. But he was arrested a long time ago, and then when he got out of prison he went into exile."

Maybe Henry had been planning a trip himself, Saul thought, and had sent him as a kind of advance team. Of course, you never knew with Gramps. He was a canny old fox, cagey when it came to getting what he wanted, and what he wanted wasn't always clear. Maybe what he wanted was to get Saul's documentary off to a running start. Or had he sent him to finish some unfinished business by proxy from Park Slope? Was he perhaps here to collect ANC terrorist loot?

Saul looked at Sipho and back at Lillian. The land was lush, wild flowers and weeds abundant in the little garden. Trees bore drooping leaves, waxy and green. Sipho pointed to the kitchen and nodded approvingly, mumbling something in Zulu.

"My grandmother bought this property from the government," Lillian said. "She built the house. Your grandfather and some other people sent her the money."

Sipho returned with another beer. "*Ooogy wawa,*" he said. "That's how we say cheers in Zulu, heh," and drank thirstily. Saul wondered about his driver, who was obviously going to drink steadily until he drove Saul back to the lodge.

Lillian had fetched a blanket from inside the house and they sat on the grass, under a canopy of trees. Dimpho busied herself with two dolls, her back to the grown-ups, moving the dolls around and whispering to herself. In a clearing, butterflies darted above the wildflowers.

"So this is where your grandmother lived?"

"After she retired, she lived here. Bought new furniture and finished the kitchen. Her sister, Leila, got a house nearby when she retired. The two sisters hadn't spent so much time together in nearly sixty years, and they had fun, like children. One would fall asleep while the other was talking; it happened all the time."

"Hah." Sipho slapped his empty Black Label can. "One of them would be talking and the other one would just fall to sleep. Jissus."

"When did you move out here?" Saul asked Lillian.

"When I got pregnant."

"So you stayed with your grandmother for a while?"

"Yes. That's why I came here."

"Me too," he said. "I mean, I lived with my grandfather. And my parents. Until I went to university." He wasn't sure that she understood what he meant.

Dimpho came up behind Lillian and whispered in her ear. Lillian smiled, whispered back, then turned to Saul.

"She wants to know if you're coming back tomorrow."

"Of course. If I'm invited."

"Yes, you are invited."

8. Blood River Day, Part I

It was decided that a simple operation would be best. Gun (black market, untraceable), gloves (no fingerprints), clothes (suit from Stuttafords, sunglasses, Florsheim shoes). Ravi Kumar only had to get close for a moment, long enough to pull the trigger. His briefcase contained a passport, documents, hotel bills—all fake. Dunningham would spot the mark; Henry would drive the getaway car.

The assassination would be the coup de grâce of a widespread, campaign—attacks on railway lines, police stations, and municipal offices that Mbeki had been coordinating with Mbede and Slovo. It would forever be known as Heroes Day, the birth of Umkhonto we Sizwe, the birth of a new nation. Come back Africa. *Mayibuye iAfrica!*

Slovo's plan, audacious to say the least, was to pull the trigger at the commemoration of the Battle of Blood River. "One shot heard around the world," he told his comrades. He laid it out for them. They were going to assassinate the Minister of Justice: Balthazar John Vorster. On the Boers' Day of the Covenant.

On that day, December 16, back in 1838, Andries Pretorius and his Voortrekkers had defended their encampment, mowing down Dambuza's Zulus as they poured across the misty fields to attack the trekkers' *laager*. The victorious Boers swore then and there to build an independent republic. A big day in Afrikaner history, and now 123 years later, there would again be a massive commemoration.

This year's gathering was to be held on the site of the battle. The day before the ceremony, Vorster would be staying in a local Pietermaritzburg hotel. The plan was for Dunning-ham to stay at the same hotel. Dressed like a local farmer in a safari suit and sunglasses, he would hang around in the lobby, waiting for Vorster's retinue to leave. Then he'd follow at a distance and phone Ravi with their location and the direction he was headed. Henry would drive to a nearby parking lot and wait for the assassination that would change the course of history. "Keep it simple, keep it small," Slovo had said.

HENRY STAYED in a nearby hotel. He slept poorly, and went down early for breakfast. He was back in his room by eight o'clock. Everything was going according to plan. He sat on the hotel bed and tried not to think about the day ahead. He thought instead about the Blue Marlin Hotel where he and Sarah had gone for dinner last summer. Their first night on holiday, and Sarah already looked tanned and lovely in a sleeveless red dress. They'd rented a house in Clansthal, and Janey babysat while Henry and Sarah ate langoustines and drank wine and laughed and kissed. That's how it was with Sarah: when she wasn't afraid of the world, he fell in love with her all over again.

The following day, Glenn and Henry had walked together along the sand, exploring the rock pools at Scottburgh beach, looking for sea anemones and shells, watching the iridescent fish and darting sandpipers. They ate ice cream in the hot sun, chocolate melting down their fingers. Henry had grilled fish on the braai outside, while Janey and Sarah cooked rice and vegetables in the kitchen. The four of them ate together at the glass table in the rental house. They could hear the thundering Indian Ocean.

It was the next day that Glenn saw the sign at the beach entrance: *WHITES ONLY*.

"Janey can't come with us?" Glenn asked.

"That's the law," Henry said. "Disgraceful, isn't it?"

"Even if we want her to?"

"Even if we want her to."

"Is that what you're fighting against?"

"What do you mean?"

"Mommy says you go to meetings to fight against apartheid."

"Well, yes. But you mustn't tell anyone. Not even your friends at school."

"I won't."

"Not anyone, ever. Promise me, Glenn."

"I won't. I promise." A quizzical expression on his face.

Henry smiled, took Glenn's hand and led him to the water. The boy swam well, and they bodysurfed and bounced around in the waves. At nearby Saint Michael's-on-Sea, they'd rented canoes and paddled up the Mhlangeni River, eventually pulling their canoes up onto a sandbank, where they stood together at the water's edge.

"What do you do?" Glenn asked. "At those meetings you go to. I promise I won't tell."

"I know you won't. What we do is, well, we make plans for a better country, with better laws. And we help people who've been sent to prison even though they didn't do anything wrong."

Glenn dug his paddles into the sand, twisting them in the spotted silt.

Would he ever tell Glenn about this day, he wondered as he waited in the hotel room. Would he ever tell him about committing crimes himself, about sitting around in a shitty hotel, waiting to be an accessory to murder?

The call came at about ten in the morning.

"He's leaving," Dunningham said. "Market Square." Just four words. Click.

Henry rushed to the car and drove to the parking lot near Market Square. The attendant waved him in and handed him a ticket, then returned to the booth at the front of the lot. Henry parked, turned off the engine. He wished he'd brought a magazine or newspaper to read, something to occupy him while he waited. He wondered if he would hear the shot. Probably. And police sirens. And then what? The Prime Minister would make a radio announcement. MK would claim responsibility, with the right tone of regret for having taken a human life. Ravi would leave the country. There would be a state funeral, possibly denunciations in the foreign media. But the ANC would weather the storm—the police raids, the glare of foreign media. *We have not embarked upon the course of violence out of choice.* The spotlight on South Africa, the fear that would descend upon their enemies, the galvanizing impact of the day, would be worth it. From this day on, all the world and all South Africans would know how serious the Struggle was and that now was the time to take a stand.

Twenty minutes passed. Thirty. Henry turned on the radio, volume low. Rugby score, the opening of a new shopping centre, Adolf Eichmann sentenced to death. He didn't want to attract any attention. A man sitting in his parked car wasn't that unusual. Still, better not to get out or make any noise. There was a bag full of cash and clothes for Ravi in the trunk. He switched off the radio.

9. Pick n Pay

Breakfast at the lodge. Saul was eating toast and apricot jam when Sipho and Lillian pulled up in the Corolla. Mrs. Zöhrer looked up from her newspaper, glanced disapprovingly at Sipho, who strode into the lobby in his checked fifties pants and Kangol cap. Saul grabbed his backpack, and Sipho called out "Good morning" a bit too loudly to Mrs. Z, who nodded and rattled her newspaper. A black youth in funny pants taking an American guest to an impoverished rural township—showing the world some poverty and neglect: what's not to love?

They drove to a big Pick n Pay store in Nelspruit. Saul's idea. Exactly what his mother would have done in the circumstances: bought some food. He pushed a shopping cart as big as a boat, and Lillian plopped things inside it. Frozen chicken, eggs, mealie meal, green beans, spinach, sausages, cookies, chocolate milk, bread, more beer. At the checkout counter, the woman in front of them—white, midthirties—was barefoot. As they stood in the queue, Lillian picked out a couple of magazines and inspected some brightly coloured princess dolls in plastic wrapping; Saul picked out a pair of black sunglasses for himself. When he paid with his father's credit card he felt beneficent and slightly embarrassed. Lillian thanked him effusively. He reddened and looked away, and they carried the groceries out to the car.

A MAN was sitting outside number 932, leaning back in the office chair in front of the house, feet propped up on the low wall, listening to music through headphones. A few feet away, Dimpho was playing with a girl about her age. When she saw the car, she jumped up and ran over. Lillian picked her up, gave her a box of cookies from a grocery bag, and Dimpho and her friend dashed inside the house.

The man watched them run, hugged Lillian, greeted Sipho, and then turned his attention to Saul.

"This is Saul," Lillian said. "This is my brother, Vusi."

They shook hands. Vusi stared long and hard at Saul.

"All the way from Brooklyn," Lillian said. And then she spoke Zulu. Saul understood only *"ugogo"* which he knew meant grandmother and "Henry Wegland."

Vusi nodded. "How's Brooklyn?"

"I like it. It's cold now, winter. Not like here."

Vusi nodded. "I would like to go to America."

Saul wasn't sure how to respond. "Yeah. Come and visit."

Lillian picked up one of the bags of groceries, and the others followed her into the kitchen, carrying the remaining bags. Saul examined the sink and plastic cistern. He felt foreign, the rich American, and wished he knew what to do or say. But making people feel comfortable—himself included—had never been his strong suit.

They stood in the kitchen, watching Lillian stow the groceries on narrow shelves and inside the fridge. Dimpho and her friend scampered through the house, then ran out the kitchen door. Saul could hear them playing at the edge of the little garden.

"You guys go and relax," Lillian said. "I'll bring some snacks."

Saul offered to help, but Lillian barred his way, a knife in one hand, an onion in the other. Sipho grabbed three beers, edged around her, and nudged Saul towards the front of the house.

"The men don't cook," he explained.

"I've seen men cook."

He smiled and shrugged. "Well, not in South Africa."

The three men sat on the old chairs in the shade and watched the dusty road. A *bakkie* loaded with people chugged up the slope, and they followed its slow progress with their eyes.

"You know, I've never seen snow," Vusi said.

"It's pretty," was all Saul could think to say. "But cold, of course."

"So what brings you here?" It sounded like an accusation.

Sipho let out a nervous giggle but said nothing.

"My grandfather wanted me to come. He knew your grandparents. I suppose he would have come himself, but he's getting old. So he sent me."

Vusi nodded, took a sip of beer. "Why?"

"He lost touch with Nellie and Ezekiel after they all left Johannesburg, and I think he wanted to come and see them, or at least get in touch again." It occurred to him that if there was a secret stash of ANC booty, Lillian's family would be living a lot better than this. No, there was no treasure trove. An old man simply wanted to make contact with lost friends. I don't want to let it go, Henry had said. Saul was old enough to understand that. Not letting go.

A shirtless boy on a bicycle rode slowly past. He paused, looked at Saul, waved at Vusi. Saul waved back.

"Yebo, Thabo," Vusi called, smiling at the kid, his don't-fuck-with-me veneer slipping for a minute.

The boy on the bike turned one last time to look at Saul, then pedalled off. Saul glanced at his bare knees. Despite the heat, he was the only person wearing shorts. He felt uncomfortable. It wasn't so much that he wanted to be black, or from there, he just wanted to be cool, to have an aura that others respected, liked. Brooklyn badass, Flatbush in the house. He glanced at his pale hairy calves, khaki shorts, Teva sandals. Cool wasn't happening.

"Some people thought maybe Ezekiel was an informer," Vusi said. "But he wasn't. He just ran away before they could arrest him."

"Maybe that's what my grandfather wanted me to find out about. Also, I want to make a documentary, a movie. About the early days of the ANC."

Sipho brightened. "I'll be in your movie, man."

They drank their beers and talked about the music they liked (Saul hadn't heard of Chronic Clan or Black Dillinger; Vusi and Sipho didn't know Radiohead or The National). Saul watched Dimpho and her friend in the shade of a mango tree as they played with the supermarket dolls. Beyond them, the valley was deep and green—almost beautiful, Saul thought, if it weren't for the furrowed road and hardscrabble houses, the poverty fringe of lush beauty.

When a car approached, slowed, and pulled to a halt, they all turned to look. The door opened with a flash of colour as a young woman climbed out. Vusi got up, gave the woman a hug, then opened the boot and took out a blue bag. The car drove off, leaving a cloud of dust.

"Ndolo," Vusi announced. "Our sister."

She was a younger, prettier version of Lillian. Dimpled, curvy, she was dressed in a denim skirt and white blouse with pink and blue flowers printed across the shoulders. She carried a silver handbag.

Ndolo hugged Vusi, who introduced her to Sipho, and then to Saul.

"Hello, person-who-wants-to-know-about-our-grandmother," she smiled.

Just then, Dimpho came running out of the house and Ndolo scooped her up and swung her around. Dimpho squealed, and Lillian appeared a moment later, a dishcloth tucked into her jeans. She kissed her sister hello, pausing for a second to take in her stylish outfit and LV bag. Behind her, Dimpho's friend stood watching Ndolo as if she were a visiting dignitary.

After a while, Ndolo put her niece down. Vusi went inside with Ndolo's bag, and the sisters chatted conspiratorially. They watched as Dimpho and her friend ran around the garden, with an occasional glance at their American visitor.

Saul turned to Sipho, who sat on the *stoep*, squinting in the sun. He had a sense of how this house usually was—busy and loud, someone cooking, someone outside, someone else chatting outside. He could imagine Nellie there among them, talking, laughing, bossing them around.

10. Blood River Day, Part II

Close to an hour, and still no sign of Ravi. It wasn't supposed to take this long. They were supposed to be driving back to Johannesburg by now. There was no way to phone Dunningham or Ravi, nothing to do but wait.

They hadn't asked Henry what he thought of the plan, only whether he would drive. Even so, after Slovo's explanation, he'd rejected the idea of killing someone. It was one thing to plant a bomb outside a building, but quite another to participate in an assassination. Dunningham said it was Utilitarianism: the moral worth of an action was determined by its outcome. Henry wasn't so sure. But here he was, part of it, tapping the steering wheel in the midday sun, tiptoeing into murder.

He had gone through it all in his head a dozen times. Ravi would receive the call from Dunningham, put on his jacket, concealing the gun and holster, take a last sip of cold coffee perhaps, or a shot of whiskey to calm his nerves. When he got outside he'd put on the sunglasses and driving gloves. He would have caught up with Vorster's party fairly quickly. Maybe the Justice Minister had stopped to pose for a photograph or gone inside a shop. How long could that take? Ten minutes? Twenty? Follow him, shoot him at close range, drop the gun, and get to the parking lot. Blend in with the crowd. Walk, don't run. The fake passport would get him out of the country.

There was a sound, faint at first, then slowly becoming recognisable—a marching band. It grew louder, brass and bass drums clamouring in the air. The band was escorting the dignitaries out of the square on their way to the site of the historic battle. Where was Ravi? The sound of the marching band faded, the horns diminishing until there was only the throb of a lone drum, and then that was subsumed by the hum of weekend traffic. So the convoy was leaving: Ravi was too late.

Uncle Isaac hadn't run from danger. He'd gone back into the fray, crossing Europe by steamship and train in 1941, despite Eva's pleading letters. They later heard from an old neighbour that Isaac had travelled first to Shadowa but, on finding most Jews gone from the place, he'd gone on to Vilnius, where he voluntarily entered the ghetto and got his ration card and yellow Star of David to sew on his coat. Henry never quite understood why Isaac had done what he did, although now, waiting in the car for Ravi and Dunningham, he felt something of the imperative that had propelled Isaac, the battle in his blood—defending a country, standing up for a people, seeing something through, staying the course.

It was nearly noon when Dunningham appeared. He climbed into the car, glanced over his shoulder to check whether the attendant or anyone else had noticed him.

"Where the hell is Ravi?"

"Maybe he's just waiting for the right time."

"No, it's too late. They're gone."

They sat watching the clock. Henry gnawed his fingernails. He turned on the radio, and listened to Radio Jukebox at low volume. "Please, Mr. Postman" and then "Peppermint Twist." Neither of them said anything for a while.

"What do we do now?" Henry eventually asked. His back ached, and he wedged a fist between the seat and his spine.

Dunningham shrugged. "Wait a bit longer, I suppose."

Sun glinted on the windscreen, and they sat together in the car, Dunningham with his long fingers draped over his knees.

It was then that Henry noticed something move in the rearview mirror. A policeman, on foot, alone. A cop assigned to the outer reaches of the parade to check parking lots and roust the hobos. Henry eased down in the car seat. *Please, no, please God no, don't let him come here.*

"Don't move," he whispered. "Cop."

11. Casa Glenn y Holly

Glenn took his time with his English muffin, spreading the jam evenly, reddening the muffin's mottled surface with the same patience Henry had observed when Glenn was a boy in Stony Brook. There, he'd folded and organised his own clothes, kept his room tidy, scooped out the cat litter, taken out the trash, and written the shopping lists. Chopin Liszts, they used to call them. Now the muffin dissolved into pools of colour, clots of red and brown, like a painter's palette. This was the visual agnosia again, playing tricks with the world. The last time they'd been to the Philharmonic—Brahms, if he remembered correctly—the stage had lifted from its moorings, the entire orchestra, splits and splays of chair legs and music stands, levitating, floating, instruments and musicians' faces, shoes, black gowns, all of it hovering and wobbly. He closed his eyes and listened and imagined an orchestra, and when he opened his eyes the visual stimuli before him were behaving properly again. He worried about a condition one of the doctors had mentioned, called prosopagnosia, not recognising familiar faces. He worried about forgetting everything, not recognising a bloody thing. Not yet. Not yet.

Holly took a sip of her tea, cradled the mug in her hands. The radio was on NPR. News from Afghanistan and Washington.

Henry was dressed and ready for his day in the city. It felt good to be busy, to have somewhere to go, people waiting for him, expecting him. He hoped to hell Glenn wouldn't bring up that damn doctor again. It had angered him to be reminded last night, chided like a child. He stared at his coffee. Damn Holly had tattled. That's why Glenn was back on the doctor bandwagon. It had happened a few weeks ago. Henry came downstairs while Holly was cooking supper. Still groggy from his nap, he'd leaned into the kitchen to say hi, asked if he could set the table. Holly said no, not to worry. Then he mentioned the CD he wanted to order. Bach keyboard concerti. He loved Bach. Stirred the soul. You could hear God in that music. His friend Joe Borgese had recommended Angela Hewitt's recording.

"Where's that boy of yours?" he'd asked. "Too busy to help with supper?" Thinking: Saul could bloody well help with supper, or order that CD from Amazon.

Holly turned from the stove. Her eyes roved across his face before settling.

"Papa, he's not here. He's back at college." She spoke gently, leaning towards him, the curious frown gone from her face.

Henry felt confused for a moment, then embarrassed. "Sorry, right, of course. Bit foggy from my nap. I meant, let's phone him later."

"Good idea." She didn't say anything more, but continued looking at him, as if she were waiting for a sign. Defect noted. Lovingly.

He'd thought that was the end of it, but then she'd told bloody Glenn. The tattletale, the snitch. That night Glenn had talked to Henry, just the two of them, in Henry's room. What had happened? What did his doctor say about these incidents?

"Nothing. It's no big deal, really. I'd just woken up. Doesn't mean I've got dementia or I'm going to start drooling and shitting all day."

Glenn didn't smile. "No, but it does mean you should talk to your doctor. And I should talk to him too. We just need to, you know, understand this. It'd be irresponsible not to."

"I'll call Silver," Henry promised. He just wanted the conversation to be over.

Now Holly sliced a banana and sprinkled almonds and granola on her yoghurt. Glenn held up two ties, and she pointed to the darker one, then went back to her granola and tea.

Mornings, Saul was always in a rush. Sleepy, mussy-haired, frantically looking for something he'd misplaced. He'd stare at his bowl of cereal more than eat it, spoon in his hand, the Cheerios like wayward life vests in a moon-white sea. Once he'd called from school. "Hello, Gramps." Just two words, and Henry knew that something was wrong, could tell that someone else was with Saul. "Are you okay?" Saul said he was fine but there was a bit of trouble at school. The panicked voice of his grandson on the other end of the line. Saul and a friend had accused another boy of planning to bring a gun to school. Henry learned the full details only when he arrived at the principal's office. Seth's mother sat with her handbag in her lap. The two boys looked ashen, contrite. They said that they'd heard the other boy whispering about a gun—wouldn't it be funny if he waved it around in the hallway or cafeteria, that kind of thing. So they went to the principal. The boy said they'd made it all up, that Saul and Seth were jealous of him, because of girls, because he was captain of the soccer team. Saul had chosen to phone his grandfather about the incident, not his mom or dad. Seth's prim mother said a few words about what a good boy Seth was, an honours student, president of the French Club, and so on. Then it was Henry's turn.

But before Henry could say anything, the principal said: "It's an honour to have an ANC activist in my office. Thank you for coming in. We'd love to have you talk to the AP history class sometime."

"Sure," Henry said, somewhat taken aback. "Of course." Then he leaned forward, as if it were just the two of them talking confidentially. He said Saul had discussed the matter with him (which of course he hadn't), and Henry had assured him that he wouldn't have to say how they found out about the gun. Henry said he should probably have been more thoughtful about his response, but he felt Saul was doing the right thing. He went on to explain that Saul was a cautious boy, an only child, that he had grown up with stories of informants and arrests and secret police. Quite right, this wasn't South Africa, he quickly agreed. Yes, no enemies here. Henry laid it on thick, blamed himself, reminded the principal that his grandson and the other boy weren't the type of kids to get in trouble. The principal nodded understandingly, said that the school had contacted the other boy's parents, and they were willing to let the matter drop. Saul and Seth would apologise. Lesson learned. The two boys went back to class. Henry thanked the principal again, then walked out of the school building with the other boy's mother. The two adults smiled awkwardly and shook hands before parting ways.

When Saul returned from school that day, Henry was waiting for him. What was that all about? Saul confessed that there wasn't any gun, nor was there any rumour of a gun. They'd made it up to get even with a rival, a bully, and they regretted it.

"Never again," Henry said. "You do something like that again and I'll personally phone those colleges and tell them not to admit you. Understand me?"

"I understand. I fucked up. I'm really sorry." He lingered in the living room, let out a sigh. He looked like he was about to cry.

Henry nodded. He was just a kid. He'd made a mistake. "You're welcome."

The boy looked up at him, incredulous and grateful. Henry could tell the boy was still surprised at how things had turned out. No expulsion or suspension. Hell, not even Glenn and Holly would find out.

"Damn, Gramps. You lied your ass off in there."

"Only for you, my boy. You know that."

"Yeah, I know that."

Glenn had finished his muffin and was putting the coffee mugs in the dishwasher while Holly packed her laptop. Henry was alone at the kitchen table when the phone rang.

From Holly's excited voice—"How are you, my baby?"—Henry knew who it was. And from her side of the conversation, Henry gleaned that Saul was giving his mother a description of a hotel, Nelspruit, his visit with Aunt Essie. They spoke for a while, then she handed Henry the phone.

"Gramps, I'm in the boonies, near Nelspruit. I found Lillian Mkhatshwa. She's Nellie's granddaughter. And Lillian's brother and sister. I don't think you ever met them."

"No, I didn't."

"Nellie's dead, Gramps. She died about a year ago."

Henry felt winded. "I didn't know," he managed, and then stood there, pressing the receiver hard to his ear. He felt like his lungs were full of fire. Waves of static and hiss.

"And Ezekiel was never really in the picture. Gramps, this place is wild, very third world." And he gave Henry a hurried description of the rural township. "So, what do I tell Lillian? Do you have a message for her?"

"Just send my condolences."

"That's it? I came all this way just to have lunch with Nellie's grandchildren?"

"Yes, I suppose so."

Glenn came to the phone. Henry heard him say, "I love you, Saul," before he hung up.

"Papa, you're in Manhattan today, right?" Holly asked.

"That's right," Henry said, still a bit shaken from the news. "Luncheon and then a meeting at Bernhard & Wallace." He liked announcing his luncheons and meetings, proud that he was still invited, his opinion still sought.

"And you're back for dinner? Glenn, we're here, right?" In this way, Holly managed the comings and goings of the family.

"Yes," Glenn said, scanning the front page of the *New York Times*. "I'm having drinks with a client. Should be back by eight, but don't wait for me."

Standing in the doorway watching them leave, first Glenn then Holly, Henry felt rather like their nanny or mother. Outside, a sea of dark trapezoids and blurry hulks drifted towards the subway with their briefcases and backpacks and caps and earmuffs. Nellie was dead. No one had told him. No last good-bye; he hadn't even been invited to the funeral. Sarah, Slovo and Ruth, Harold Wolpe, Rusty and Hilda, Govan Mbeki, and now Nellie—all gone. He felt a great sweeping sadness for them, and for himself, for the holes in his heart, the chasm that was his past, that was South Africa, the floating world without people to moor it. He stood there and waited for the shifting shapes to become people, and for the cars to morph into cars again. Then he went upstairs and put on a suit and tie.

12. DEEPER, DARKER

They fed Dimpho, sitting on a blanket under the mango tree. Her little friend had gone home, and now she turned her attention to the grown-ups; she clambered over knees and shins, pressing her face and fists into her mother and aunt with an odd seriousness, as if she were conducting a secret experiment. From time to time she looked up at Saul. He wondered what they'd told her about him, the American, the interloper.

After a while, Lillian picked Dimpho up and carried her inside, followed a few minutes later by Ndolo. Saul stayed outside with Vusi and Sipho, who were slowly drinking their warm beers. A couple of houses away, a radio was playing *kwaito*; down the street some kids were kicking a soccer ball.

"Man, have you seen this China's cell phone?" Sipho said, pointing his beer can at Saul. "iPhone."

Saul handed the phone to Vusi, who clicked through some apps. Was he scrolling through Saul's music collection? Looking at his photos? At Claire, the beautiful redhead from his dorm, who couldn't give two shits about him, even though he was madly in love with her? It was a crush, a stupid infatuation. He'd taken the photo when a group had gone to see a play on campus. She was never going to go on a date with him, let alone have sex with him.

Vusi handed back the phone, and Saul showed him a picture of his grandfather and a few shots of New York—a bar in the East Village, Brooklyn Bridge, Prospect Park. When

Saul got up and went inside to use the bathroom, he found Ndolo in the living room, checking messages on her phone, and asked if there was a picture of her grandmother and mother. She picked up a framed black-and-white photo from the sideboard. Nellie as a young woman, tall and beautiful, standing beside an older man; her father, Saul presumed. Ndolo pointed out other photos: Nellie holding a baby; Ndolo's mother and father, she in lace with sparkly earrings, he in a tuxedo.

"Where's your mother now?"

"She passed. Long time ago. When we were in school. She got pneumonia, and by the time they got her to hospital, she was in a coma."

"I'm sorry."

She showed him a photo of their mother sitting with her three children in a garden. Another picture was of a young man with big glasses, wearing a suit and tie.

"Simon," she said. "Nellie's eldest. We never knew him."

Saul wanted to ask her more about Nellie, but he couldn't formulate the right question. He looked out the window at the *stoep* and the green land and felt a vague sense of loss— for Nellie and Lillian's mother and Simon, for the dead and exiled, and for his documentary that seemed to be losing shape like some menacing ghost, briefly appearing and then floating away.

Ndolo went back to the kitchen and Saul joined the men outside. Vusi was on the phone again; Sipho was leaning back against a cinder block column, eyes closed.

Blue sky, clouds like taffeta. Saul thought about his grandfather, and smiled to himself. Most college-age kids, most of Saul's friends anyway, didn't really like their grandparents. Not Saul. He liked his Gramps. Even though Henry was short-tempered, quick to criticise, a snitch, and a card cheat. A few days after they'd moved into the house in Brooklyn, Henry shouted at Saul: "We mustn't forget the revolution," and "Nothing endures but change." He kept at it like a crazy person for ten minutes before breaking into a smile and patting Saul on the head. A vocal critic of green vegetables, bad wine, American football, presliced cheese, anything in an aerosol, his Gramps also hated tofu, video games, hooting, litter. He liked dirty jokes, theatre, *South Park*, quoted Shakespeare, Malcolm X, and Richard Pryor. ("I don't know what it is, but I'm going to fuck it," was his favourite Pryorism.) Not your average grandfather. He told his grandson masturbation was good, and he should have all the sex he could—using protection, of course. People said they were alike, although when they said it Saul wondered how alike a Brooklyn teenager and a Lithuanian-South African octogenarian could be. But they played chess together and rode bikes in Prospect Park, and when Henry went to visit him at college they skipped the museum and walked instead to a pub where they played darts.

Dimpho waved and said "hello" and Saul smiled and waved back when Lillian brought her outside again. Vusi bounced her on his thighs. The child laughed and tugged at his earlobe. Seemed to have a thing for ears. After a while, Vusi handed her to Sipho, who took her finger and walked around the garden. She squealed and jumped about, and then Sipho led her back and put her hand in Saul's, and Saul led her on another circuit, around the front of the house, in and out of shadows, on and off the grass, then back again. "Hiya doing?" he asked. She looked at him blankly, but smiled and tugged his hand.

Ndolo breezed past, then paused. She was going to visit Nellie's sister, Leila. Would Saul like to come along? Saul returned Dimpho to her mother, then walked with Ndolo along Modisana Road to another narrow dirt road, with the same ramshackle row of matchbox houses. A few had small chicken coops, some had fenced-off gardens, and one had a goat tethered in the tiny backyard.

"Did Nellie's sister also know my grandfather? Was she in the Struggle?"

Ndolo laughed. "Leila? No, she stayed in Breyton. Nellie, she was married before, but that guy was no good. A *skelm*. That's why she left. She ran away to Joburg."

Leila lived in a house higher up in the hills. A lean woman with a broad gap-toothed smile. They said hello, Ndolo chatted with her in Zulu, and then they left without going inside the house. Things were different, Saul realised, because he was there. They were being really nice to him, all except Vusi, who seemed to view him as an annoyance. But the sisters were certainly putting themselves out, talking to him, showing him around. After Leila, they visited another friend, a young woman about Ndolo's age. She didn't say much to Saul. Like Leila, her English wasn't very good. Mostly she and Ndolo gossiped and laughed, and when Ndolo gave her a blouse she'd bought in Johannesburg, she clapped her hands and kissed Ndolo and ran inside to try it on.

"I don't think Vusi likes me," Saul said when they were walking on the road again.

"He doesn't dislike you. That's just Vusi."

"A hard case."

"A nut case?"

"Hard. A hard nut."

She smiled. "Yes, he's a hard nut. But soft on the inside. It's his job, you know. And it makes Lillian safe here. He's Mapogo."

"What's that?"

"Mapogo is kind of a private police force. Good-guy gangsters. People fear him and they stay away from his sisters. So we're safe. He says it's like the old ways. People had respect. When people did some crime, they usually confessed, out of respect. Vusi says we have to go back to that."

"People turning themselves in?"

"Respect. Community. In the old days, if you confessed, handed yourself over, there would be less punishment. Still not good, though. They would tie a person down on an ant hole. Red ants. Very painful."

"What about the police?"

"Hah. The police are shit. They don't worry about the locations. They can't even keep up with crime in Nelspruit."

"So Vusi is like a citizen police force? Like the Guardian Angels? Has he ever shot anyone?"

"No, not Vusi. His job is information. Two cell phones, no gun."

"Two cell phones?"

"He says telecommunications is power. One is for top-secret business, so the police can't trace the calls. He says President Obama has two cell phones."

"I guess that's true. Vusi want to be president one day?"

"Maybe. Why not?"

They walked in silence for a while. Saul's skin prickled with sweat; he kicked a rock. As much as he liked being with the Mkhatshwas, he hoped to be back at the lodge in time for a swim.

His family always told him that Gramps had taught him to swim. This would have been Cape Cod or Amagansett. Saul didn't remember, and couldn't really imagine it. Impatient, irascible Gramps. Muttering when he taught Saul to play chess and backgammon: "No, Saul. You can't move there." *Gaunt move theh.* Of course, there was also the proud, supportive Gramps. Whenever Saul did well on a test in school, it was proof of something larger. "He's got a very sharp mind." That was his ultimate compliment. And it worked. His parents told him stuff like that, too, but when Gramps said it, he believed it and something like pride ballooned inside him.

Mom was always bragging about Gramps, hoping in this way to draw him into conversation. Usually this happened when talk turned to South Africa, and Mom would say something like, "Henry knows Nelson Mandela," or "He was at Rivonia, you know." For a while, she'd added, "That's like being present at the signing of the Declaration of Independence." Gramps would glare. "Rubbish. It's nothing like being

present at the signing of the Declaration of Independence."
End of conversation. That was Gramps. People seemed to
piss him off. A lot.

"Your grandmother, she sounds like an amazing woman,"
Saul said to Ndolo.

"Ag, ja, hey. Our gran was a champ."

And Ndolo proceeded to tell him a bit about Nellie—grew
up on a farm, taught herself to read and write, moved to
Johannesburg where she worked first as a maid then as an
assistant at a chemist's, joined the ANC, stole supplies to
build bombs, ended up a deputy director of the Gauteng City
Parks Department. She'd also managed to buy the house in
Ka Nyamazane, put Ndolo through school at Parktown Girls,
and hold together her far-flung family.

"We're all a bit lost without her, for sure, but she was
happy, you know, so that's the best comfort."

Saul got the impression of someone who had worked
hard, lost a lot, and clung to her granddaughters with a fierce,
tenacious love.

"She had a lot to be proud of," he said.

They passed a peach-coloured house, larger than the
shacks around it. A single palm tree grew in a patch of grass,
and a car stood in the driveway.

"And what about Ezekiel? What happened to him?"

"Zeke? He stayed in exile a long time. He went to China
for military training. Then Tanzania. He helped train a lot of
ANC guys."

"He came back, though?"

"Yes, he came back. He and Nellie stayed together then,
but not for long. I don't know what happened. I was young,
and we didn't see much of him. One day he went back to
Port Elizabeth, and she didn't go with him. He was a big shot,
on the Executive Committee of the ANC. He passed maybe
ten years ago."

With her Joburg accent and easy manner, Ndolo might
have been gossiping with a city girlfriend, although every

time he looked up at the unfamiliar surroundings or down at his legs and sandals, he felt every bit the *uitlander* again.

"Nellie never remarried?"

"No. She had a boyfriend in Johannesburg. Wilton. But she never talked much about him either."

"Why don't our grandparents like to talk about stuff like that?"

Ndolo laughed. "Who knows? As Nellie used to say, Don't trouble me with old stories."

"Sounds just like my grandfather. They don't want to go back into the past. I'm not sure why."

"Maybe they want to go back, but they just don't want to take us with, hey."

THEY ATE fried chicken and salad on paper plates, sitting on a blanket in the shade. Then Saul said, "I've got an idea. Is there some place around here we could buy one of those little plastic pools? Wouldn't Dimpho love that?" He was thinking of his grandfather teaching him to swim, of doing a small, good thing.

"You don't have to—" Lillian began.

"If he wants to," Vusi interrupted. He pointed to a patch of shade. "There, we'll put it under that tree."

13. Blood River Day, Part III

Henry turned off the radio, eyes still on the rearview mirror. He was aware of Dick's breathing and the smell of someone else's car—damp, human. He watched the cop walk up and down the row of parked cars. Felt a quiet hatred for the man. Maybe he wouldn't notice them. Maybe he'd check a couple of cars and move on. What if the shot rang out now? What if Ravi came running into the parking lot? The cop didn't seem very interested in the cars, but nonetheless made his way dutifully along each row. Soon he was close enough for Henry to see his thin face in the mirror, a millimetre of blond stubble visible below his black cap, right hand on his baton. Their eyes met. Henry rolled down the window.

"Good afternoon, officer."

"Afternoon."

Henry didn't have a fake driver's licence or passport. Ravi did, but not Henry or Dick. What would they do if the cop asked for his licence? Drive off? Shoot him? There was a gun in the cubbyhole. Not bloody likely. Submit to questioning, probable arrest? He could feel the blood in his head, swooshing around his temples.

"Hello, officer," Dunningham said.

"Gents." The policeman was standing at Henry's open window. "Mind opening the boot for me?"

A surge of panic. Stay calm. Breathe. "Yes, of course."

Henry pulled the keys out of the ignition. Opened the door and climbed out on wobbly legs. The sound of their shoes on gravel warbled in his ears. He made a mental list of the trunk's contents—his bag and Ravi's. What was in Ravi's BOAC bag? He couldn't remember. A change of clothes and a tin of paraffin. In his own bag was a map of Pietermaritzburg, dirty socks, and underpants. What else? But his mind was uncooperative. He kept coming back to the gun in the cubbyhole. Was he ready to kill a man at close range? Could he do it? If it were a matter of saving his own life? But it wasn't a matter of saving his own life. Nor was it like planting a bomb. You pulled the trigger and the man in front of you was alive one minute and dead the next, an explosion of blood and burned flesh, brains and gunpowder and death, and some of it spattered your arms and face. His hand shook as he turned the key. Was this how it would end? A random car search, arrest, interrogation. Would he be strong enough to divulge only the names of people in exile or known informants? Would Dick? He didn't want to go to jail. An image of Glenn flashed before him—wiry legs in his school uniform. Gun, cubbyhole. Maybe he could use it as a threat, get in the car and drive off, take back roads or abandon the car and hitch?

He pressed the knob and the boot swung open.

The young cop bent forward, glanced at the bag, the tin of paraffin, rags, spare tyre. Henry was close enough to read the name tag on his pocket—Blauer—and the knobs on his walkie-talkie. No gun, thank God.

Henry concentrated on breathing. "Everything all right?" His own voice sounded tinny, distant. Where was Ravi? He hoped to hell he'd stay away just a few more minutes. "Our wives have gone out together," Henry ventured. "We're just waiting here, catching up on the rugby scores." He was babbling suddenly, like a bad actor. "Vrystaat keeps winning, I'm afraid." Christ, he sounded like a Pom or a Joburg *windgat*, not the good-bloke-*landsman* tone he sought to affect.

The cop leaned forward, picked something up. A photostat of the Justice Minister's schedule Henry had tossed into the boot. Then he pulled the envelope from Ravi's bag, opened it. Moçambique passport, wad of cash. He straightened, adjusted his cap.

"I'm going to need some identification."

"Yes, of course," Henry tried to sound nonchalant, cooperative. His throat felt hot and tight. He could hear the policeman's walkie-talkie crackle as he walked to the driver door and opened it.

"What's going on?" Dunningham hissed, gripping the edge of his seat.

"He's seen the passport, the money."

"Shit."

Henry opened the cubby, took out the gun. Dunningham flashed him an astonished look but Henry was already walking to the back of the car.

"Corner of Klip and Market Street," the policeman was saying.

It took him a second to register the gun in Henry's hand, and when he did he stopped speaking.

"Switch it off."

He turned off the walkie-talkie, slid it back into the plastic case on his belt. "I don't want trouble."

Dunningham was out of the car now. Henry looked at the street, the parking attendant's hut. There was no movement.

"Get in the car," Henry said, slamming the boot shut.

Dick opened the back door and the cop climbed in.

"Here, take the gun," Henry said to Dick. "Sit in the back with him. We'll drop him off on our way out of town."

Dunningham took the gun and climbed in beside the cop.

The car rumbled to life, gravel crunching under the tyres. A vertiginous feeling, as if he were floating in the air above the car. He didn't slow down as they passed the surprised parking attendant and pulled onto Market Street.

In the rearview mirror he could see Dunningham staring sideways with the gun against his thigh, aimed at their hostage. Blauer was unnervingly calm, and Henry wondered if he'd been trained for hostage situations.

Chatterton Road was a straight shot out of Pietermaritzburg. Traffic was moving well, and they passed slow cars, a lumbering Scania lorry, *bakkies* ferrying day workers. Henry pulled onto a dirt road.

The negotiation was very fast. They gave Blauer all the money they had—including Ravi's considerable escape fund—and took his walkie-talkie. They told him they knew his name and if anything happened, they would come after him.

"I understand," the cop said.

"This never happened," Dick said.

"Ja, it never happened." He straightened his cap and started walking away.

They passed him on their way back to the main road, and then they were heading back to Pietermaritzburg.

"You all right?" Dunningham asked after they'd been driving a few minutes.

"I suppose so." Henry looked ahead at the tar and featureless landscape.

"John bloody Wayne."

"What was I supposed to do?"

Dunningham took out the map. "My God. How long before they start to look for the car?"

"Dunno. Twenty minutes? Should we ditch it?"

In the end they decided not to abandon the car. There would be fingerprints. They might also be recognised from the policeman's description if he called it in. They stopped at a hardware store and bought screwdrivers and a spanner. In a hotel parking lot they stole the licence plates off a car from Pretoria. Followed back roads towards Johannesburg.

There was nothing more they could do now. Henry would get the car back to Yusuf, and with a bit of luck he would be able to keep it off the streets a few days longer. Yusuf knew the owner personally, and he could be persuaded to provide false information if the police inquired as to the whereabouts of the car on December 16. *You must be mistaken. The car was right there in my driveway.* At worst—no, worst was too bad to contemplate. Worst was a day or two more of freedom before they went to prison. The evidence was irrelevant. If they connected them to Ravi or Umkhonto we Sizwe or bloody anything, then they'd be tried for treason or sedition.

The streetlights glowed like burning husks against the afternoon sky. The road dipped and rose and dipped again below the tree-lined horizon. He would take the car back to Yusuf. That's all he could do now. And then he'd go home. He wanted to take a bath, to hold his son. He wanted a whiskey, bed.

14. FIFTH AVENUE FREEZE-OUT

A luncheon at the University Club. "Globalisation, Innovation, and Capacity Building in Southern Africa." Cosponsored by the University of the Witwatersrand and the Wharton School, underwritten by Deloitte and several law firms. Henry rode the subway to Fifth Avenue. Collected himself before entering the Moorish building with its vast lobby and doormen in grey suits. Upstairs, he was given a nametag, pencil, and Cleary Gottlieb notepad by a very young-looking woman, then he entered a large room already buzzing with conversation. Got himself a cup of coffee. An associate from Bernhard & Wallace introduced himself. It felt good to be back in the fray, back in his element. Once a month or so he attended some kind of event—a panel at the UN, lunch at one of the law firms he used to do business with, a speaker at a club, someone's retirement party. He still went out to Stony Brook, still had dinner with friends and old neighbours once in a while. Henry Wegland had no shortage of friends or quasi-business dealings. He took trains and cars and rode the subway into Manhattan, and generally kept himself occupied. Good for the mental faculties, good for the soul.

Lunch was buffet style. Standing before the steaming silver servers, a young man asked Henry what company he worked for. When he told him he was a retired law professor, the guy seemed to lose interest. Young people. He was probably trying to network, land a client, or get himself a new job.

Professors from both institutions spoke briefly, then answered questions, mostly agreeing with each other about green entrepreneurialism, free trade zones, China's role in southern Africa. Poached salmon, wild rice, soggy zucchini. There was little in the way of speculation or debate, mostly a lot of talk about the financial crisis and its effect on Africa. The questions were too long, Henry thought, and the professors spoke in circles. The result, for Henry, was the sensation of listening to a simultaneous translation. Also, the room was hot and he was thirsty and he couldn't reach the jug of water in the middle of the table.

When laughter rippled around the room, Henry realised he hadn't been paying attention. He was usually interested in these things, but today it all seemed a bit of a bore. Perhaps it was something he ate. Or was it the place, the tenor of the event, the nagging feeling that he was unnecessary, an old timer, of no interest to the professors and young professionals, most of whom had probably never set foot in South Africa and couldn't find Zimbabwe on a map. A historical curio. It was not a role he relished. He didn't like their shiny clothes, their showy ties, the way they were always checking their phones. What about change? What about action? That's what really got his goat. Their bourgeois insouciance. What about the violence? What about one in three South African women in their twenties living with HIV, or the second highest murder rate in the world? What about that? There was still so much work to be done. Real work, not accords on green energy, not task forces. The country had come so far, no question, travelled a long road from despair to hope, darkness to daylight. South Africa was a land of change, of freedom. And yet. When they had dared to dream a future in the tremulous early days of the Struggle, it had shone far brighter than the mottled, benighted present. Today's townships were the same horror show of unemployment, degradation, and violence they'd been forty years ago. Okay, better plumbing, electricity, paved roads, whole neighbourhoods of middle-class splendour, but forty percent of township residents were unemployed. Fanon's endgame was a daily reality: the last battle of colonised against coloniser is the fight of the colonised against each other.

Meanwhile, corruption flourished at every level; it permeated daily life. The oligarchs and venal first families, construction, public works, mining, police, local government, even Armscor and Denel—the state-owned defence companies—were all a tangled web of corruption. A scourge. Meanwhile, apartheid-style repression seemed to be making a comeback. New laws proposing sweeping changes threatened to quash freedom of speech and usher in a new era of silencing anti-government critics. The Protection of State Information Bill. People were already calling it the "Secrecy Bill." Disgraceful. Information needed freedom, not protection.

Not that he had given up. Henry still had hope, still had faith. You don't give up on something you love. You can't. The future was always brighter than the present, Henry thought. Because the future was a dream, not a destination. But no one wanted to hear about it, not here, and so he ate his salmon and sipped Chardonnay and pretended to listen. Nellie was dead. *Ubuso obuhle*. Beautiful face. Beautiful spirit. She had lost so much, Nellie, and borne so much. Another comrade gone. History had scattered them over the earth. Time had made them old. Or dead.

The room felt uncomfortably hot. The salmon tasted like chalk. He tried again, but still couldn't reach the water jug. After a few more questions and a few more ripples of laughter, the thing at last began to wind down. Someone thanked everyone for coming. Waiters swooped in with trays and began plucking plates off the table.

People milled about, exchanging business cards beneath the soaring windows and shaking hands with the speakers. It was only when Henry began to make his way out of the room that someone paid any attention to him. A Bernhard &

Wallace associate, a woman with short black hair, wanted to know if he was coming to the meeting afterwards.

"Yes. Just going to get a breath of air."

"Okay. There are cars downstairs." She glanced at her watch. "We'll leave in about ten."

"See you down there."

Henry shook the woman's hand and hurried out. He knew he looked totally out of place among the busy professionals who were checking their cell phones and quickly exiting the luncheon. But what did he care about appearances, about the opinions of a roomful of strangers? More than anything, he wanted to feel cold air on his face, breathe in great draughts of it.

He took the lift downstairs, crossed the wide marble lobby, and got himself out on the street, where he joined the throng of tourists winding along Fifth Avenue, past the narrow chocolate shop and the NBA store ablaze with colourful team jerseys and video monitors. A few tourists paused to take photographs; busy-looking business people swerved around them, shouting into cell phones. Down the avenue cars were hooting; taxis idled at the intersection, billowing exhaust fumes. Cars and people and noise, and whirling flashes of yellow and black and grey. The air was refreshingly cool. Henry loosened his scarf and tie, unfastened the top button of his shirt.

Engulfed by crowds at the intersection, he knew there was something else he needed to do, somewhere he was supposed to be, but there was a stronger impulse, to walk, to breathe. He would have run if his old legs could have carried him away from the people, out of gravity; he'd have liked to jump, to soar above the pedestrian bustle. Then the light changed, and people rushed forward, surging around him, and for an instant it was all too much, the dizzying yellowness and skeltering people, flashes of light and asphalt, here a bike messenger, there a blur of legs and shoes and boots, black and blue shapes. A car hooted, then the world went watery and flickered and he heard a sound like birdsong in his head, glimpsed a quiver of sky, then a sudden quiet, like when you switch off a radio, only not quite silent, and he felt something like a great wave pound him, and he crumpled. The wave pulled him down into the misty greyness of the street. A moment of blackness, the street hissed, blinked, the sidewalk tilted. Car doors floated by, a rush of trousers and shoes, another belt of the horn, as a taxi driver, a lanky Indian man, leaned out of his window and shouted, "Asshole motherfucker," before pulling back into the traffic.

Henry found himself sitting on the pavement of Fifth Avenue, between the gutter and passing cars. Up close, the road was more grey than black. Rubber-threaded asphalt, a foil cigarette wrapper. A taxi passed close enough for him to read the decal on the yellow door: *$2.50 initial charge.* His hip throbbed, and his heart was pounding. The street blinked. Everything was suspended, everything waxy and slow. He had the sensation of swimming, of rising up through water, the light diffused and murky, surfacing through shadows and echoes, as the volume rose again, blare and blur, and the street swam into focus—busy, spangled—a bus, potholes, a hot-dog vendor, a big glass doorway. Someone was helping him, tugging him upright.

"You all right?" A young man, not much older than Saul.

Another man, a security guard, perhaps from the glass-fronted store, rushed onto the street.

"You okay?"

"Yes, I think so."

The boy hunkered beside him, locked his hands under Henry's arms, and the security guard took his hands, and together they hoisted him upright.

"You sure?" the boy asked.

The few steps across the sidewalk were difficult. Henry felt dizzy; his right leg shot with pain. He had trouble putting weight on it. When they got to the wall, he let himself sink into the smooth cement, and there he rested.

The young man was looking into Henry's eyes. Was he a doctor? No, too young.

A wave of nausea hit him. He put his head down and squeezed his temples. When he opened his eyes he wasn't sure how much time had passed. He knew he'd been hit by a taxi, but he couldn't remember how it had happened. Stand up, he told himself. Keep it together. A small crowd had gathered around him, and he watched them gradually disperse. A young boy turned back to look at him, holding his mother's hand. Henry noticed a manhole cover, the small rubber tyres of the hot-dog vendor's cart.

"Want me to call an ambulance?" the young guy asked. "Or 9-1-1?"

"No, I just need a minute. Catch my breath."

The security guard was walking back towards them. Henry heard him say something but couldn't make out the words. He was talking to someone else, a cop, who approached Henry and the young man.

"Cab just blindsided the old guy," the guard explained. "Then took off."

The cop nodded, scratched his ear. "You want to file a report?"

"No. I'll be all right." His voice sounded hollow. Like it was coming from the bottom of a giant tin can.

The guard and the boy looked at each other, shook their heads.

The boy had curly black hair and round cheeks. Dominican or Brazilian maybe, Henry thought, noticing his frown of concern as he looked from Henry to the cop, then back at Henry again.

"Okay, let's get you inside," the cop said.

They flanked him and walked him into the Gap. He tried to keep his weight off his right leg, gritting his teeth as he hobbled into the store. There was loud music playing, too loud, and the smell of vanilla and plastic. The guard disappeared for a moment and returned with a chair. Henry happily sat down. The nausea had subsided, but hot needles of pain moved up his back and down his thighs. He felt exhausted.

Someone brought him a plastic cup of water, which he drank in two trembling gulps. A pretty girl in a red T-shirt had come over from the cashiers and stood looking at him. Her name tag said Tianna. The cop was on his walkie-talkie. The young man hovered nearby, uncertain what to do.

"What's your name?" Henry asked him.

"Lionel. I work over in the Saint Regis, in the kitchen."

"Thank you, Lionel." It was Saul's middle name, Rusty Bernstein's given name. "You've been a great help. There's no reason for you to stay, though."

"You sure you're okay?"

"I will be. A bit dazed is all. And my leg hurts like blazes."

Lionel smiled. "Hurts like blazes. I never heard that."

15. Heroes and Blood

"The cop who saw you, you're certain he doesn't know your names?" Standing in the doorway in his double-breasted suit and pale-yellow tie, Rusty looked rather dashing. He also looked tired.

"Yes, quite certain."

"But he could pick you out of a lineup?"

Henry winced. "Yes. Hopefully he didn't call in the licence plate."

Sarah appeared, gave Rusty a kiss hello, and asked after Hilda. Glenn followed them into the living room, then tugged Rusty towards his room to show him his model airplanes and drawings. When Henry knocked on the door, Rusty commended the precision of Glenn's drawings and mussed the boy's hair before following his father downstairs to the study.

They'd received word from a source, Rusty said. Ravi had been arrested. That's all he knew. Henry explained the situation with Yusuf. Their fate may be in the hands of the car's owner who was, Yusuf said, not a sympathiser but a good bloke. Yusuf hadn't phoned, so presumably the owner hadn't contacted him. And maybe that meant the police hadn't contacted the owner—and maybe it didn't. Henry had worried himself sick about this until he'd simply given up, exhausted by his anxieties about probability and luck, fate and God and kismet and grace.

"Not very much you can do," Rusty said. "Lie low, keep away from everyone for a while. No meetings, no contact."

"Sure. Of course." It was almost a relief to be told to stay away.

Rusty touched Henry's shoulder, and they walked to the window.

"Listen, if they'd connected you with Ravi or traced the car, you'd be in jail by now."

For the most part, Blood River Day had been a success, Rusty said. Umkhonto had blown up an electrical substation in New Brighton, telephone lines in Port Elizabeth, a Bantu administration office in Alice, two police stations, railway lines, a bus depot. Five explosions in Port Elizabeth alone. Only two arrests: Rex Luphondwana, who had thrown the petrol bomb in Alice—and Ravi.

"Stay for some supper, Rusty?"

"I'm afraid I can't. Have to get going," he said, standing up. "Our love to Hilda."

That evening the fear and self-recrimination returned. Henry sat alone, couldn't even play with Glenn, and cursed himself for his stupidity, or ineptitude, or hubris. Who was he kidding? He'd made the same mistake every petty criminal makes: I won't get caught, not this time. Also something like shame. Rusty was soldiering on. Govan and Slovo, too. They all were. Prison, refugeedom, or freedom: those were the options. Courage wasn't the absence of fear, Nelson said, but the triumph over it. Henry had read Emerson: A hero is no braver than an ordinary man, but he is brave five minutes longer. Henry felt very ordinary.

HE COULDN'T sleep. Woke up thrashing, grinding his teeth. Watched Sarah beside him, envied her serene sleep, her body warm and thick with it. Ever since Pietermaritzburg, he hadn't been able to sleep through the night. Rusty was right, of course. There'd been nothing on Ravi's person and he hadn't talked. Yusuf would keep the car out of circulation a few more days—the best he could do—in case the police were looking for it. The beat cop probably hadn't filed a report, otherwise he'd have been arrested by now. But still, Henry didn't feel safe. Just because they hadn't found anything yet didn't mean they wouldn't. A cop had seen him. With paraffin, cash, a fake passport, Vorster's programme. Maybe the money had been enough to buy his silence. Or maybe they'd already pieced things together and were just waiting, watching him, to see if he might lead them to a bigger fish. He couldn't discuss things on the phone with anyone. Sarah knew some of it, and guessed from his behaviour that something had gone wrong. She was angry at him for doing whatever it was that he couldn't tell her, he could sense that. But she'd put her arms around him and stroked his hair. Now, in the middle of the night, he wanted to tell her everything, but there was no point. There would only be more for her to deny or lie about if the police ever questioned her. And if they came for him? He wanted to be ready. He lay awake and stared at the dark outlines of trees in the grey-black sky.

A few days later, Rusty sent a note to Henry's office, buried inside a legal document. Ravi had taken poison in his prison cell. Henry spent the next hour staring at his desk, and most of the afternoon in the office toilet, retching.

Dunningham stopped by that evening. Made a big show of returning a tennis racquet he'd borrowed. They walked in the garden, and Dunningham told him what he'd learned from their police contact via Slovo. Ravi had arrived as planned, had navigated his way through the crowded high street. When Vorster's retinue turned left into Klip Street, Ravi ran across the road to follow them. That's when a policeman noticed him. At the intersection, the two men collided, and when Ravi fell, the cop saw his holster and gun.

That night, Henry kissed Sarah and held her tight and told her that he loved her. Later, he tiptoed into Glenn's room where the boy lay sleeping, wiry legs outspread, arms akimbo. Henry leaned over and kissed his head, felt the hot short breaths on his cheek. He backed out slowly, and as he stood in the doorway watching his son sleep, tears welled in his eyes.

THE POLICE didn't knock on the door the next day. Or the next. Life went on. The Struggle ate its way into his legal work, with the consent, if not blessing, of Briggs, Fleming, and Pfister. One day, over lunch on Simmons Street, Duncan Callan talked sotto voce about a new case. Bespectacled, brilliant, and an old friend, Callan worked mainly on a number of pro bono cases for black clients. The defendant had been banned, ostensibly because he was in the ANC and a member of the Communist Party, but in truth because of something that he had published in *Drum* magazine about an incident in one of the townships where police had assaulted and shot people attending a funeral. One man's head was smashed so violently that his brain oozed with the blood onto the road. Henry listened to Duncan's concise summary of the case's merits.

They ate veal, drank a glass of red wine. A bourgeois lunch for revolutionaries, Henry thought. The bourgeoisie had been corrupted by a government whose weaponry included capitalism and inertia, and if those didn't work, there was a massive, repressive police force and secret service. The revolution would wage a war on people's souls. Then power would pass from one hand to another, from a fascist hand to the people's hand, white capital to the working class. In secret meetings of the underground Communist Party, they had discussed Lenin's rules for revolution. A mass organisation that could communicate with the workers, coordinate nationwide activities, unite all social strata and maintain unity and secrecy, while raising money and mobilising foreign governments. No mean feat. Oliver Tambo was their one-man band abroad. It was impossible to tell if the majority of the country was in fact on their side, if contact and communication had been established, if the rest of the world would bother at all. How could they win the war when they were too scared to mention Lenin's name in a restaurant? This had long been Sarah's fear—the sheer might of the enemy. They had jails, a police force, a subservient justice system. They had laws and informants and tear gas and torture. They had guns.

They talked some more about the case. Henry told his friend that he thought it was a good case, a winnable case. Duncan smiled, took off his glasses, and rubbed his eyes. "They keep inventing new laws and cutting the balls off the old ones. They'll probably ban *Drum* next, then all of this will change."

They were having their coffee, the restaurant half empty, when Duncan leaned forward. "What about you? I won't be called upon to act on your behalf, will I?"

"Me? No, I'm fine."

Duncan's eyes registered a flicker of doubt, or fear.

Henry paused, contemplated his coffee cup. The searing truth flashed only for a moment, like now, when he considered what it might mean to escape, to run from a far more powerful foe—or to lose, to get caught. He had a burning desire to know how it would end, but knew that this would be denied him. Could he endure prison? He didn't think so. What did it feel like to hang? He was gripped by an intense sadness, and felt suddenly old, like someone in a science fiction movie, *zap-pow*, and they landed in the future. He'd seen *Invaders from Mars* just a few weeks before. *The work at the plant is secret. We have orders to report anything unusual.*

HENRY WORKED on the trial with Duncan. He enjoyed the research, poring over past cases, reading about banning laws and freedom of information, the new laws that gave the Prime Minister sweeping new powers. But after about two weeks the trial was postponed because of another appeal before the Supreme Court. No way of telling whether the postponement was legally sound or the result of a crumbling legal system.

Summertime. Evening swims. After work, Henry kicked the soccer ball with Glenn. Ndimande watered the garden and mowed the lawn. Sarah played bridge on Tuesdays. Henry drank more than he used to. They went to dinner parties, weekend bring and braais—friends around the pool, cold beer, and plates of sizzling *boerewors*. Work went on. Henry drafted briefs and contracts, then revised, revised, revised. He looked around, saw others his age blithely content, making their way in the world. But family, security, kipper and eggs for breakfast, scotch and soda in the evening were not enough for Henry.

Days passed by, and still he wasn't arrested. He got dressed, ate breakfast, and drove to work. And the days became weeks and Henry grew more assured. He started sleeping better. The Dunninghams threw a big New Year's party. Brian Pfister said 1962 was a good year for Claret— he'd bought six cases of Bordeaux futures. Weeks went by. And then it was a month. Every precaution had been taken. For all the police knew, Ravi had acted alone. Henry was just beginning to believe his luck, to believe Sarah, when one morning the doorbell rang, and two policemen were standing outside.

16. A PLASTIC POOL FOR DIMPHO

They were talking about who would go, and where to buy a plastic pool for Dimpho. The hardware store on the way to town probably stocked them. If not, then Pick n Pay or Price Mart in Nelspruit.

"Pick n Pay," Vusi intoned in a TV baritone. "Inspired by you."

"Maybe we'll pick up ice cream and beer," Sipho suggested.

"Yebo," Saul flourished one of his three Zulu words. He picked up his sunglasses and went outside to wait for Sipho.

Ndolo was holding Dimpho, swaying her from side to side, holding her upside down then right side up. "Wheee."

Just then the noise of a car. From his perch on the *stoep*, Saul watched a Honda bump down the rutted road and pull to a halt. The engine revved, then switched off. A puff of dust settled behind the rear tyres.

The passenger door opened, and a skinny man climbed out. He took a few steps towards Saul, nodding, looking straight at him.

"Get inside the house," the stranger said.

Then he said something to Ndolo in Zulu, and she turned round, lassoing Dimpho.

The driver got out of the car. His large shaven head glinted, streaked with sweat; his pale-green shirt bulged at the belly. Ambling towards them, he pulled something from the waistband of his jeans.

An eruption of Zulu from the skinny guy. His eyes were small black marbles; his thin moustache a smudge above his mouth.

Ndolo scurried inside, carrying Dimpho. Saul looked up, saw what the bigger guy was holding: a gun. He felt his jaw snap shut. Gun. He looked at it again. Still there. His mind went blank. He followed Ndolo inside.

The living room was quiet. Vusi and Lillian stood together on the far side of the room. Lillian wrapped her arms around Ndolo. Sipho stood just inside the front door, still holding his car keys. The skinny guy spoke slowly in Zulu, while the big guy locked the front door, pulled the blinds closed, then locked the kitchen door. He walked around the room and took everyone's cell phones. He examined Saul's phone briefly, then dropped it in a brown plastic bag along with everyone else's, tied the handles, and hung the bag on the front door handle.

Vusi spoke in Zulu, but the big guy just pulled a face and shook his head: No fucking way. No one moved. Motes of dust hung in the air. Everyone watched nervously. The big guy sat in the armchair, gestured to Vusi and the two sisters and little Dimpho to sit on the brown settee. Saul watched them squeeze into their assigned seats, then sat down on a chair. Dimpho murmured, started to say something, but Lillian pulled her close, silencing her. Saul noticed the fleur-de-lis pattern of the settee's fabric. The gun barrel was grey and scuffed, the handle wood or fake wood.

Fat Man, obviously the leader, scanned the room. He said something to Skinny Guy, who just nodded. Lenny and George, Saul thought. Nip and Tuck. Tweedle Dum and Tweedle Dee. Hustle and Flow. And then he stopped making up names and went back to being scared shitless.

"Okay," the big one said to Saul. "Now you do what we say." He pulled at the collar of his green shirt. He looked at the others and gave an instruction in Zulu. Vusi nodded, raised a hand as if to say, cool, no problem. Saul nodded too.

Scotch and soda. Simon and Garfunkel. *When you're weary, feeling small.*

The big guy glared at Saul. "Get your ATM card."

"Okay." He turned to Lillian. "I need my backpack."

A more concentrated wave of fear coursed through him. He saw now what they all were: hostages, victims waiting to happen. Who knew if Fat Man and Skinny Guy were high on something, or if one of them was a psychopath, a killer. More than anything, he wanted not to be there, to be safe—at home, at college, in a place where he knew what was going on, what would happen next, where he was in control, somewhere there wasn't a gun a few feet from his head.

"We put it away." It was Vusi who spoke. "In the bedroom."

Fat Man nodded, gave an instruction, and Vusi rose, started towards the bedroom. Saul followed. He felt heavy and puny at the same time. His chest tightened around his heart.

Fat Man didn't move, but muttered something to his accomplice. Bridge and tunnel. Dun and Bradstreet. Done and dusted. Vusi made his way down the hallway, followed by Saul and Skinny.

The bedroom curtains were closed, and a faint perfume hung in the air, rosemary maybe. He couldn't see the backpack.

Vusi said something to their assailant, then bent down beside the bed. "I stuck it under the bed," he said, "so that Dimpho wouldn't find it and have a go at your things."

Dumb and Dumber. Dead and deader.

Saul bent down beside him, and for an instant he blocked Skinny Guy's view of Vusi, who whispered, "Take your time, man. Go slow."

Saul saw what was in Vusi's hand—another cell phone. *Telecommunications is power.* Saul's throat tightened, and his eyes went dry. They both moved slowly, patting the floor underneath the bed as if it were completely dark under there. But Saul could see the backpack quite clearly.

"Such a lot of crap under here," Vusi said, followed by some words in Zulu.

"*Kamsinyane*," Skinny Guy grumbled. "Hurry man."

Saul saw the bottoms of his black jeans, his new Adidas sneakers.

"There it is," Vusi said.

Saul slid slowly from under the bed, his chest against the cement floor, breathing hard. Vusi was grunting. A filigree of shadows cast by the curtains and window bars wobbled and settled.

There were two bricks under each foot of the bedframe, there to lift the bed out of the reach of *tokoloshe* and other evil spirits that lurked at night. But either the bricks had failed or these *skelms* were a different kind of spirit, because here they were, inside the house, waving a gun around and demanding money.

"Okay," Vusi grunted. "Got it."

He pushed the backpack across the floor. Skinny Guy picked it up. As he pulled himself up, Saul saw two things— Vusi's thumb punching a button on the mobile phone and Skinny unzipping the backpack.

Vusi pulled Saul towards him as Skinny unzipped the backpack. "Listen," he whispered, his face centimetres from Saul's. "Nedbank in Nelspruit. Main branch. Don't go to any other branch. Okay?"

Saul nodded.

When he stood up, Skinny waved Saul's wallet in the air and slung the backpack across his shoulder. Vusi stood up, and they made their way back to the silent living room.

17. Home with Holly

Henry sat in the back of the police cruiser as they sla-
lomed through afternoon traffic on the West Side Highway.
The river slipped in and out of view, the Jersey City skyline
twinkling in the window. Lionel had called the Saint Regis,
and they'd offered a courtesy car, but the police officer had
already called his precinct and a cruiser arrived in minutes.
Henry, of course, didn't want to go with anyone. He could
make his own way home. He'd been getting home, getting
himself out of scrapes, for the better part of eighty-four years.
He'd suggested they drop him at Glenn's office, which wasn't
far, near Union Square. But they insisted. They would take
him home to Brooklyn, or to a hospital.

So here he was, in the back of a police cruiser, like a perp,
a grimy plastic partition between him and the officers up
front. They passed the piers, the Hustler Club, the towering
Standard Hotel, bikers and joggers.

"You doing all right back there, pal?" The one in the passenger seat turned briefly. He had grey hair, was older and
plumper than most NYPD, Henry thought.

"I'm fine."

They took the Battery Tunnel, descended below the
southern tip of Manhattan and sped through the oneiric darkness. The lights inside the tunnel fused and blurred, then
unblurred. Up and out the other side, Brooklyn, back into
the Technicolor day. On Hamilton Avenue, a truck was block-
ing traffic. They passed warehouses, a low-income housing

block. All his energy had oozed out of him, and Henry leaned back against the stiff vinyl seat. He wanted to be somewhere still and quiet. Usually he was the one who did the rescuing, and he thought of that day at the beach, the day he'd met Sarah, all those years ago. He'd been there with Merberg. Their freshly laundered towels, the white sand, wide blue sea. They'd been watching a group of young women nearby, watched as two of them stepped into the frothy water, giggling, waving their arms in the hazy sunshine. A few minutes later, a sound roused them, one of the girls nearby was shouting. She was pointing, shrieking, waving her arms at a flailing figure far out in the surf.

Fourth Avenue was busy. Cars rushing and hooting; steam rose from a subway pipe. The double-thump heartbeat of a manhole cover. They passed a tyre repair shop, a clapboard house, its empty clothesline a dark stripe against the sky. His leg had gone stiff, and a hot searing pain pulsed through his right buttock and across his lower back. With the shaky enervation came a feeling of helplessness, as he sat in the back of the police cruiser and watched Park Slope whirl past the grimy window. He didn't want to be a doddering old man, didn't want to end his life in some old-aged home in Westchester.

He swam strongly, through the salty spray and churn, point A to point B, straight as a ruler, and when he was close to the young woman, he called out to her. And then he was upon her, close enough to see drops of water on her pale cheeks, a lock of red hair under a floral swim cap. A wave swept him up and away from her. Her arm—slender and pale—reached for his as they paddled closer again, each with an arm outstretched, like shipwrecked ballerinas. The water tilted and shifted, but the waves were still for a moment, and he was able to grip her arms. Her eyes were red from the sting of seawater. She was close, her face inches from his own. Her hand gripped his shoulder. They fumbled for a second, her hands slapped waves, slapped Henry. Too shy to grab her by the waist, he tried to take hold of her shoulders, but realised that would push her down into the water. He adjusted his grip again, inching her forward along his chest. His wrists and fingers skipped across flesh, the cold fabric of her bathing suit, her ribs, before he was able to get a grip with his right arm and hold her afloat. It helped that she was clinging to him. He began to kick steadily, swimming towards the beach. They hadn't progressed very far when she slipped away again. He shifted, wrapped an arm around her waist—to hell with propriety, she was drowning—and kept kicking. They were moving now, waves washing under them and sometimes helping them along. When they were close to shore, Henry was able to bounce along on his toes. It was then she asked his name. "Henry," he said. And in that instant, a whiff of rosewater floated up from the brininess. "Henry," she repeated, then coughed. "Thank you, Henry."

THE POLICE cruiser pulled up outside the brownstone. The cops wanted to see him inside, but Henry insisted he was fine, thanked the men effusively. They waited anyway. He could feel their eyes on him as he unlocked the door with shaky hands and turned to wave good-bye.

The entrance hall calmed him. Safe at last. There was a coat hook in the hallway, but Henry never used it. Up the carpeted stairs, into the quiet embrace of the house, with its smell of wood and lemony kitchen cleaner. Later he would come down and drink a cup of tea and read the newspaper. Pain shot down his leg with each step as he climbed past Glenn and Holly's floor.

He heard a noise before he had ascended the last stairs to his own floor. A riffling sound like leaves blowing in the wind, followed by a low rumble that sounded like a human voice. The door of Saul's room was open, and inside was Holly sitting on the bed, leaning against the wall, her legs dangling. Seated beside her was a man Henry had never seen before.

They were both untucked and shoeless. He found himself staring at their toes. They looked like children who'd seen a ghost. Holly's face and neck were flushed. A bra, or what looked like a bra, lay on the floor at the foot of the bed.

"Henry." Holly was the first one to speak.

Having said his name, however, it was clear Holly couldn't think of anything salient to add. She looked up at him, then over at the man sitting beside her, then shook her head as if in answer to a question the man had posed sometime before.

"Yes," Henry replied at last.

He didn't have anything else to add, either. How are you? Who are you? Neither question seemed quite right. Nor did anything else. He noticed that the window was open, felt the crisp air that entered the room. On the window sill sat a battered tin of mints and a book of matches.

He looked at the man. Bushy black hair, blue eyes, handsome in a pudgy way, vibrant blue shirt, hands at his sides. Holly blinked, chewed her lower lip. Above her, the eye-stinging geometric pattern of a rock band poster.

"I was just showing Jonathan around the house." Holly stood up, smiled at Henry.

"Hello, Mr. Wegland."

"Hello."

Was there a strange smell in the air? The tin, the matches. Henry turned and, without saying anything further, continued to his room. He closed the door behind him and sat down on his bed.

AFTER THE man left, after Henry had taken two painkillers, drunk a glass of water, sat in the armchair in his room and considered the sky for a while, he got up, put on a cardigan and slippers, and walked down the hallway. He paused outside Saul's room. What was Holly thinking? Here, in her son's bedroom? The window was still open a crack. The same sweet smell in the air. It took him back to Washington Square,

Gerde's, Joe Borgese's lopsided grin from a booth at Kettle of Fish, student parties at Stony Brook. But this was Holly, this was now. He turned and padded downstairs.

"Hello, again," Holly greeted him, half turned around on the sofa.

He stood in the middle of the living room. He hadn't thought about what he would do or say. He still felt befuddled from the accident, woozy. In the window, the branches looked like purple shoelaces draped across the sky. Holly's head was a fuzzy brown planet hovering above the couch. Henry sat down.

"It's not what you're thinking," she said.

"I'm thinking everything."

It didn't come out as he'd intended. He meant that he was thinking about the accident and Glenn and Sarah, not just about Holly and what she had or hadn't done today. He'd meant to say something that would calm her, put her at ease, but his words only served to agitate her further, and now they sat there, mute and stiff, occupying chairs they didn't usually sit in, not looking at each other, twitching and fiddling.

"You're home early." She was frowning. "I thought you had a lunch and a meeting."

He felt a quick wave of crossness. He hadn't done anything wrong. She was the one in bed with a strange man, dammit. But calmness prevailed. "I wasn't feeling well." He didn't want her to leave, didn't want her to flee this encounter. "Truth be told, I got hit by a bloody cab."

"You what? Henry, what happened?"

"I was crossing the road. Taxi blindsided me. Nothing serious, just knocked me arse over gob."

"Oh, God, are you all right?"

"Yes. I think so. I'll be stiff as a plank for a few days."

"Let me take you to the doctor. Or the emergency room."

"No, I'll be fine. Really. Nothing a scotch and a couple of painkillers won't cure."

"You sure?" She began to get up.

"I'm sure, Holly, really–"

She sat down again. "Damn cab drivers. They should be more careful."

For a minute neither of them spoke, and he took in the pangaeic hum of Brooklyn—traffic, electricity, bits and bytes and millions of sound waves and atoms aloft above Park Slope, aswirl in the sky.

"Who was that?"

"Oh, God." She sighed, let her head fall into her hands. "That was my friend Jonathan from work." She looked supplicatingly at Henry. "What can I say? That I've been unhappy? I have. It just happened. And I feel like shit. I know I've done something terribly wrong. But–"

"I'm not the one who's going to accuse you."

"What does that mean?"

"It means I'm not the one who is wronged here. I wouldn't dare to judge you or tell you what to do. And I won't tell Glenn."

Now the first tear leaked from her eye. "Oh, Henry," she said quietly, letting the tears fall.

He got up from his armchair. When he approached, she recoiled slightly, then let him stroke her hair.

"Who among us . . ." he whispered. He touched her face, then returned, somewhat painfully, to the armchair, and sat down. He was exhausted, a tiredness deep in his bones.

She was crying freely now, wiping the tears with the back of her hand. "Oh, Henry, don't be all fucking perfect and understanding. I'm not sure I know how to deal with that."

"You'll deal with it." It was the kind of thing Saul would have said. He thought about the boy now. They mustn't tell him—he almost smiled as he thought this. Poor Saul. All he could think about was getting laid, and the only person having sex—in his bloody bed, *nog*—was his mother.

18. Kantoor van die Magistraat

Henry had a busy day ahead of him. The Highlands Brewery deal had hit a snag, and Glenn had a cough and either he or Sarah might have to pick him up from school. But all of that melted away when he saw the two cops at the front door.

"Morning, sir." They looked like teenage Afrikaner kids, fresh out of the academy—scrawny, pimpled.

"Can I help you?"

One of them scratched his nose, proffered an envelope.

Henry opened it and removed an official-looking document. The seal of the *Republiek*, vellum paper, *Kantoor van die Magistraat*. "Whereas I, Johannes Balthazar Vorster, am satisfied . . ." He read it through with the cops standing in front of him. He had to remain within the confines of the house and garden, and there were details as to how and when he was to appear at the Magistrate's office to receive further instructions. The reason wasn't clear, but the reason didn't need to be clear. It was simply a way of disrupting your life. They had squashed him. With a little bureaucratic flourish, a simple document signed by J. B. Vorster, Minister of Justice.

Henry watched them drive off. Then he put on his tie and jacket and drove to the Magistrate's office. Sarah called his secretary, told her about his detention, and asked her to courier the brewery agreement to the house.

THE MAGISTRATE'S Office was in Marshall Square, Johannesburg's police headquarters, a brooding brick building. Inside, typewriters clattered and phones rang. A bored desk sergeant produced a ledger and took Henry's details, then told him to sit in the waiting room across the hall. Four rows of hard green chairs. Henry stared straight ahead, held his briefcase in his lap, looked at the clock on the wall, the door that rarely opened, and told himself it was much ado about nothing—nothing more than bad luck. Sarah had remained calm when she'd seen the orders. He would cope. Nelson was coping with living underground, with being a wanted man. "The struggle is my life," he'd written the year before. "I will continue fighting for freedom until the end of my days." The words gave Henry some resolve. Do not go mad, do not run, do not surrender, just sit and wait, he told himself.

A portly Deputy Magistrate with short bristly hair called him in half an hour later. Henry submitted his request that he be allowed access to the law firm where he worked, delivered a brief summary of the deals he was working on. The dour official didn't seem at all interested. Shut him up with a flick of his pen.

"We have your information, Mr. Wegland," he said. Henry would receive a letter from them shortly. Until then he was not to leave the house without written permission. Of course, written permission had to be applied for, and this would take some time. "You are free to go," the Deputy said.

Free was the one thing he wasn't, Henry thought. Did he use that word on purpose?

He drove home. He was under surveillance: monitored, constrained, banned. He was on a list. Did they do this before they arrested you, or because they couldn't arrest you? He couldn't think straight. His head was empty, an echo chamber. He wanted to shout; he wanted to know what they knew. His panic was tinged with regret—had he put his family at risk, ruined his life?—and also a cold hatred for the people who had done this to him.

He SPENT the next day in his study. He read the newspapers. No mention of any arrests. He resisted the urge to pick up the phone. A courier delivered a folder, and he spent much of the afternoon revising the brewery purchase agreement, drafting a memorandum about restricted stock and how to handle minority shareholders. Although he found it difficult to concentrate, it felt good to do some work, to get out of his head and dig into contract clauses, skimming through related agreements, jotting down notes and answers to the client's questions. His presence seemed to make Janey uneasy as she went about her daily routine, and she peered into the study rather nervously. Sarah brought him tea, leaned over, and held him close. "Don't worry," she said. "This is just a scare tactic. We know that. If they had any evidence, they'd arrest you. They've got nothing. Probably spotted your car at a meeting, that's all."

He phoned Dunningham at the University. Careful, in case the phone was bugged, speaking as Dick's lawyer, which he wasn't, but it was a good cover.

"There may be a delay in the legal matter we're handling for your family."

"A delay?"

"Just a legal snag. Also, I'm afraid I've received official instructions limiting my movement. I'll need to apply for permission to attend the meeting with your accountant."

He heard Dick inhale sharply. "Not to worry," he said after a while. "Thank you for calling."

That evening, Dunningham stopped by with the lease for a building his father owned on Anerley Road. To make it look official. In case the phone was bugged, or the house was bugged, or someone was spying on them.

Henry poured them both a drink and they sat out in the garden with its pleasant summer sounds.

In low tones, Dunningham said that there was no reason to worry. He'd spoken to a lawyer, an Afrikaans solicitor who had frequent dealings with the police. He'd made a few phone calls, found out what he could about the house arrest. There wasn't much to discover. Most likely Henry had been connected to the Party, spotted at a SACP meeting, or identified in a photograph. They'd have to wait and see if there were other house arrests or searches. But they both knew that the police might be watching, waiting for Henry to lead them to his MK contacts. They both knew that if they were linked to Ravi, they'd be *diep in die kak*.

THE SCHOOL called to say that Glenn had a fever, and Sarah went to pick him up. Dr. Trager phoned in a prescription for her to collect at the pharmacy. Henry felt the anger of impotence, understood the masterstroke of restricted movement, how clearly it said, *We control you.*

Janey ran Glenn a hot bath, then bundled him up and put him to bed.

Downstairs, Henry and Sarah argued—about Dunningham's lawyer friend, about Glenn's cough and his homework, even about supper.

Henry went to check on Glenn, sat on the bed with him, felt his forehead and the glands in his neck. He stood up, examined the bookcase, and asked if he'd like it if they read a book together.

"You choose, Dad. Why are you home from work? Mom says you're not sick."

"No, I'm not sick." He pulled *The Old Man and the Sea* from the shelf. "Ever read this?"

"Mm, sort of. I started it."

Henry looked at his son. "I'm home, well, because the government has restricted my movements. Do you know what that means?"

"I think so. Like you did something wrong, so you have to stay home. Like detention."

"Sort of like that." He sat on the bed. Glenn's legs were curled up under the blanket. "Not wrong, exactly. They just don't like what we're doing, Mommy and me and people like us. They don't like us telling them the government is wrong; they don't like us trying to change things."

"So you think *they've* done something wrong, and they think *you've* done something wrong?"

"I suppose so, yes. They don't want to change."

"But change is good?"

"Yes. Nothing endures but change." He mussed the boy's hair, damp on his clammy forehead. "*Old Man and the Sea*?"

"What's it about?"

"An old man—"

"Ja, and the sea. Duh. What's it really about?"

"An old man and a fish, I think. And a boat. Why don't we start? If you don't like it we'll try something else."

"Okay."

Henry picked up the book. The cover, a woodblock print in stark green and black, depicted a hunched old man and a slender boy facing a churning sea.

Henry climbed onto the bed beside Glenn, plumped a pillow and put it under his head before he began to read: "He was an old man who fished alone in a skiff in the Gulf Stream and he had gone eighty-four days now without taking a fish."

It was strange being home all day. He wasn't sick and it wasn't the weekend. It took awhile to sink in just how much his freedom had been curtailed. He was, for all intents and purposes, a prisoner. He owned the prison, he had the key, but he was not free. He worked in the study and spoke on the phone to clients and colleagues but had trouble concentrating. When he wasn't working he tried to read in the living room, picking books randomly from the shelf, but nothing sustained his interest for long.

It took him back to his childhood. Staying indoors, the memory of his mother knitting in the living room, watching the world through heavily curtained windows and muttering imprecations. *Don't go far. Be back before supper.* He was just ten years old that first year in Port Elizabeth, with no friends his own age and no Uncle Isaac to whisk him off for a day of adventure. So Henry walked the streets alone. Sometimes he got lost and his heart quickened for a while, but he always found his way home. He began to go farther afield, walking from their house all the way to the shops on Moore Street, though he never bought anything.

He hadn't predicted this aloneness when he'd sat beside his father on the deck of the *RMS Saxon* and imagined his new life in Africa. A group of boys assembled daily on Lewis Road, playing marbles or shouting *"Skop die blik!"* as they dashed around. Henry kept his distance—aloof and alert. His mother kept Mikey inside, and without his little brother beside him or his uncle's companionship, Henry felt invisible, as if he were floating and no one could see him or touch him or see the things he saw. On the streets he saw shiny automobiles, black women balancing bowls of fruit on their heads, sailors in their blue-and-whites, and darkly tanned Afrikaner women in town for a day of shopping. At home he read books and out-of-date magazines his father brought from work. Soon he would go to school, his parents promised. And they would move to another place, and buy him a bicycle and smart shorts and *velskoens* like the other boys wore. Meanwhile, Mikey busied himself with eating, burping, and shitting, Eva busied herself with Mikey, and Jakub spent his days working and planning a better future for his family.

T*HE LETTER* that arrived five days later contained the details of his banning orders. Same thick paper, Kantoor van die Magistraat. Henry was forbidden from attending lectures, parties, demonstrations, theatre, cinema, or any gatherings of more than four people. He was not permitted to leave the magisterial area of Johannesburg, nor could he visit any black area, township, or factory. Communication with any banned or listed persons was prohibited. He was allowed to go to the office, and he could visit clients approved by the Magistrate's office, as long as he was home by six thirty. Any other meetings or business trips required an additional request, which could be made by phone. A response would be delivered, within a week, signed by the Chief Magistrate.

He went to see Briggs, whom he had known ever since his clerkship, and who had been one of the main reasons Henry had joined the firm. He closed the door behind him.

He explained the details of the magistrate's orders, and began to apologise, but Briggs cut him short.

"Troubled times," his mentor said. "It must be very hard. For you and Sarah. We take freedom for granted. As we should. As everyone should. Okay, leave it to me. I'll speak to some of the younger lawyers and phone a few clients personally."

"I'll get everything done, of course," Henry said. "And I can meet with existing clients, just not large groups."

"We'll manage, don't worry." It was the closest he'd come to indicating his approval of whatever it was that Henry had done to get himself into trouble. "Go home. Be with your family."

"Thank you. Thank you very much." Henry felt like hugging the man.

There were one or two clients who knew, clients who would provide cover for Henry to have meetings with comrades while appearing to be taking care of their legal affairs. One such client was Colin Beswick, an investment manager who lived and worked in a large house in Dunkeld. He was raising money for the Great Mineral Fund, and Briggs, Fleming, and Pfister were writing the agreement. It so happened that Colin was an ANC supporter, had helped to arrange visits with foreign dignitaries, and provided the guest cottage behind his house for comrades in transit. Ezekiel Mkhatshwa had stayed there for two weeks before flying to Lobatse, the Bechuana-land border town that had become the destination of many ANC exiles. Now his wife, Nellie, was living in the cottage.

Nellie was in hiding, and Henry was only allowed to travel during business hours and could only visit a proscribed number of places, so they had tea together when Henry went to Colin's house. Other than occasional conversations with Colin and his gardener, this was Nellie's only social interaction. And she was the only comrade Henry saw, other than brief social visits with Dunningham and a few hurried meetings with Rusty. So they were comrades, Henry and Nellie—but more than that, they shared the new loss of freedom. Their lives were narrowed, paths blocked. A watched man and a wanted woman. Henry would say hello to Colin, make a phone call or two from the spare room, then slip out through the kitchen and knock on the door of the cottage, sometimes with a pot of tea or a jug of lemonade.

"Wanted by the police, and I end up with my bum in the butter," she said. That smile again, the schoolgirl shyness.

They made each other feel better, safer. They would endure, as would so many others. And if they endured they would win, eventually. She touched a finger to her mouth when she smiled, as if she were trying to hold the smile in place. When he glanced up and caught her unaware, looking out the window, he saw someone beautiful and vulnerable and sad and strong, and hoped she would still be there the next time he visited.

HENRY AND Sarah devised a plan—what they'd do if the police picked him up. Most of the comrades had plans. Some would certainly be picked up; some would go to jail. The only question was who and when. Their plan provided relief from the constant fear, and gave them something to do. Sarah would demand to see the papers. But keep calm: don't give them the satisfaction of a breakdown. That would only draw them back, like hyenas circling the weak. She would phone one of three lawyers on the list, telephone Henry's bosses. Notes would be slipped inside loaves of bread, in the spine of a Bible or hardcover book if he were imprisoned. If the warder allowed bread and books through the prison gates. If.

19. BAD SHIT RISING

The fat one stood up, gestured for Saul and Sipho to leave the house. When he spoke to Saul it was with a look of disdain so fierce that Saul felt certain he was about to be spat on or punched or kicked in the nuts.

"We're going, man," he said. "We take you to the bank machine. You get the money and come back here. You run, you shout, you try any fucking thing and I will shoot you dead. Understand?"

"Yes, I get it."

Skinny Guy settled in the armchair, gun on his lap. Everyone was still, even Dimpho, who sat on her hands, staring at her feet.

"Okay, let's go."

So this was the plan. Skinny Guy would guard the prisoners, while Fat Man took Saul to an ATM. As Saul walked to the door something unfurled inside him, something swift and sharp that made him feel faint. He tasted bile in the back of his throat. Here it comes, he thought. Bad shit rising.

THEY CLIMBED into Sipho's Toyota, Saul in the passenger seat and Fat Man seated squarely in the middle of the backseat, his broad face filling the mirror, his big purple lips in a sneer. He reached around the back of Saul's headrest to lock the passenger door, barked a Zulu instruction, and Sipho put the key in the ignition.

"Joko Tea," the radio sang as the car started, "gives you strength when you need it."

Sipho switched off the radio, and they started off down the bumpy road.

Fat Man spoke to Sipho, but all Saul could make out was "N4." Sipho gripped the steering wheel; not once did he look at Saul.

On the N4, billboards swept past them. Saul thought about unlocking the door when they came to a stop and making a run for it. But now he couldn't do anything, now they were speeding along the highway. His hands were sweating, his feet were sweating, his balls were sweating. They wanted money. That was all, wasn't it? He'd give it to them, then they'd all go home. Or Vusi's good-guy gangsters would swoop in and save him. He kept thinking of *The Godfather* and *King of New York*. But this was different, this was commonplace South African theft. Happened all the time. He'd read about it, heard Gramps talk about it. A country of fifty million people with more than sixteen thousand car hijackings a year, a murder rate higher than in the US. What they didn't tell you: how many of those carjackings ended with the jackee getting killed? Blood surged in his head, and he couldn't seem to get enough air into his lungs. It took a few minutes for him to calm himself. Panic wouldn't help. Jumping over the seat and trying to wrestle the gun from Fat Man woudn't help either.

Traffic was moving well. As it probably always does when people are being carjacked or robbed, Saul thought. When you're late for a flight or rushing your pregnant wife to the hospital, that's when there's a sudden traffic jam at two in the afternoon. But get in a car with a guy with a gun, and there's no traffic to speak of. Trees and billboards rushed by in a blur. Saul wanted out, wanted to punch the man, put a gun against the back of his head and see how he liked it. He wanted to open the door, to get away—only they were going too fast, and there was a gun somewhere in the vicinity of his kidneys, and he had to believe the guy who said that if he made a run for it he was dead. Rural South African highway. One gunshot. No one would notice. They'd dump him on the side of the road.

Sipho pulled into the left lane, then onto an offramp. The outskirts of Nelspruit: Shoprite, Steers, a video store, dry cleaner. Some older buildings with wooden columns and peeling paint.

How had this happened? Just terrifically bad luck? Or was Sipho in cahoots? Not that it really mattered. Of course, if Sipho knew nothing about what was happening, he'd be more likely to protect Saul. If he was involved, then maybe he had done it too often to care about the hostage. Besides, he'd been drinking beer all day. He was drunk. He was calm and drunk, and no one had said they were going to shoot him.

Fat Man spoke, and Sipho slowed, put the blinker on.

They turned left, passing a hotel that could have been modelled on a saloon in a Western movie. Saul thought again about making a run for it when they slowed down. He could unlock the door, jump out, and roll. You had to roll when you exited a moving vehicle. But he didn't want to get shot, didn't want to die. Not today.

20. Beautiful Hands

An afternoon meeting with Colin Beswick. Afterwards Henry walked with Nellie in the garden. At the back of the property, half hidden by trees, near the neighbour's wall, stood an empty fountain shrouded in vines. A blue semi-circular pool ringed with shiny silver-green tiles, like fish scales. Henry and Nellie sat on the low fountain wall, facing the garden, their backs to the overgrown wall and dry spout. At the far side of the garden, pink pincushions dotted the green shrubs.

"We never grew flowers when I was a girl, only vegetables," Nellie said.

"Where was that?"

"Breyton. Do you know it?"

"No."

"You wouldn't. I was three before I saw a white man." She looked around. "Where are we now? We're in no-man's-land."

"A very pretty no-man's-land," Henry replied.

SOME DAYS later, Henry took two Lion Lagers to the cottage. Nellie opened the door, wearing a black skirt and a white cotton shirt.

"*Sawubona*, Henry."

"*Sawubona*." He held out the beers. "Can I buy the lady a drink?"

"I think you already did."

Long slender face, dark eyes, skin the colour of dark choc-olate, her short Afro soft and sheeny. Henry had never seen a black woman this beautiful up close before. In meetings, at Ezekiel's side, she'd always been a comrade, someone else's wife, and maybe, yes, he wasn't accustomed to looking at black women that way. What way? Beautiful, desirable.

They walked in the garden, then sat on the fountain wall and drank their beers. She told him she spent most of her days reading. Dickens, Harold Robbins, Fugard's new play, *Blood Knot*. Colin had a good library and she availed herself of it.

They sat in the dappled shade looking across the lawn at the jacarandas, shrubs, and pincushions, the lilac sky. An old wheelbarrow stood beside the garage wall.

"So peaceful here," she said. "It's hard not to want every-thing to stay like this. Don't you think?"

"Do you mean that rich whites don't want things to change?"

"I meant here, this house. But I can understand their fears, their feelings, can't you?"

"I think equal rights are more important than pretty gardens."

She laughed, low and warm, covering her mouth with her hand.

"The land shall be shared among those who work it," he said.

"These freedoms we will fight for. Side by side."

Side by side. A promise, a prayer.

She leaned back, tilted her face to the sky. Henry could see the silky brown skin of her neck and her clavicles and shoulders.

"Where are you from, Henry?"

He told her what he remembered about Lithuania and Liverpool, and she described her village near the Swaziland border. Her brothers had been herd boys. Her father had worked for the Roads Department. Henry could smell the minty scent of her hair as they talked about their children. Nellie's daughter, Thandi, was two years older than Glenn, and Simon was in high school. They'd grown up in Breyton with Nellie's parents. After Nellie moved to Johannesburg, she saw them once every two or three months at most. She took them presents—books or clothes for Simon, a doll for Thandi—and they all helped her father with his small parcel of land, planting seeds or harvesting the mealies. But they were older now, living in Alexandra township with Zeke's sister, so that they could attend a proper school. Recently, she'd been able to see them more often. That is, until Zeke went into exile and she "disappeared."

They showed each other photos, Glenn bare-kneed in his school uniform, sitting on a stone wall at Saint John's, Simon in his black glasses, little Thandi in a white dress a size too big. Henry said maybe the children would meet soon. Nellie smiled and said, Yes, maybe.

"How much have you seen them, since moving here?"

"Once."

"That's not a lot."

"No, it's not. But I'm used to not seeing them very often. It's how blacks must live in this country. We are robbed of our families—not just our land, liberty, and human rights."

"You'd better amend the Freedom Charter."

She laughed.

They watched the sun sink into the trees. The last of the jacaranda blooms were drooping, dark as grapes, and every time the wind blew a few more tumbled earthward.

"You can't risk seeing your children because you might get caught," Henry said.

"It would be dangerous for them, but also for the cause. We can't think only of ourselves."

"So you wouldn't be seen with me."

"If I was seen with you, everyone who saw us would be suspicious."

"I know. But it might be nice to go somewhere else with you, other than this house, this garden."

"What's wrong with this garden?"

He didn't answer.

"We can't," she said. "You know we can't."

He told her about his years at university, the law firm, trips he'd taken, places he wanted to go. She told him about her decision to leave Breyton, taking the bus to Johannesburg with all that was important to her in a secondhand suitcase. He watched as she spoke—the movement of her mouth, the tiny striations in her lips—mesmerised by the sound of her voice. The thrill of looking at her fingers, or the splash of freckles on her cheeks. Watching her, he felt a brightness bursting inside him.

He touched her hand then. Just three fingers on top of hers. Felt a tingle as her fingers stroked his.

"Beautiful hands," he said.

"Izandla ezinhle."

"Izandla ezinhle," he repeated.

"Ngiyabonga."

21. CIRCLE OF LIES

"**I** don't know how it happened. Does anyone ever know?"

"I . . ." Henry began. "You don't need to explain."

"You don't set out to have an affair. One day you're friends with someone, enjoying their company, you know, having a nice time together, and then slowly . . . you don't even know it at first. It just happens, becomes something else. I'm not saying you're powerless to stop it, just that it takes you by surprise. I mean, unless you're one of those people who sets out to do something like that. Which I didn't. I absolutely didn't. And then, after it's happened, you, I . . . just didn't think about it. When I wasn't with him, with Jonathan. I couldn't."

They were in the living room, with cups of tea. Holly tugged at her hair, pushing it behind her ears.

"Do you know what I'm saying? Do you think I'm a bad person?"

"You're not a bad person. You're a good person. A lovely person. You know that's what I think."

"I'm not sure if everyone is going to think that."

Henry didn't know how to reassure her. His loyalties were not divided; he was loyal to both of them.

"Can I ask what you plan to do, if you're planning on leaving Glenn?"

"No, I'm not. God, no."

Henry had the urge to hold her and tell her everything would be all right, but instead he just smiled at her. "Good. That's good."

She took a sip of tea, then held the mug just in front of her lips. She bowed her head like a penitent, and he watched her put the mug down, a tremor in her hand. When she looked up again she was crying silently, tears falling from red, swollen eyes. Henry perched painfully beside her on the couch, and put a hand on her shoulder. He fished his handkerchief out of his pocket and dabbed at her cheeks and the rivulets of mascara.

"It's okay," he said, and when he had dried the last of her tears he put his handkerchief in her hand. "It's all right."

She sat quite still, blotted her face with the handkerchief, and after a while took his hand and pressed it against her cheek.

"You won't tell Glenn about that accident today, will you?" Henry asked after a while.

"No. I probably should. But under the circumstances. Saul told me you lied to get him out of trouble at school, by the way. I do know that."

Henry shook his head, smiled. "Little bastard. Swore me to secrecy."

They sat side by side with the branches swaying in windows. So there it was, Henry thought, their circle of lies and half-truths. Holly would lie to Glenn, Henry would lie to Glenn, Henry had lied to Holly and Glenn. Saul had lied and then told the truth. Glenn didn't lie but he didn't tell the truth either. Though, who among them did?

22. SOUL TWIST

*F*riendship 7 orbited Earth three times and landed in the Atlantic Ocean near Bermuda on a clear February day in 1962. Henry and Glenn listened on the radio, and the next day they huddled over the newspapers, examining the photographs, reading the captions and statistics. The spacecraft circled the Earth at seventeen thousand miles per hour before parachuting into the ocean. "That was a real fireball," John Glenn told mission control. Glenn considered it his very good luck to be the astronaut's namesake, and he and Henry began peppering their conversations with phrases like, "Roger that," and "Reading you loud and clear." Sarah smiled and shook her head. Henry's house arrest would last another hundred and sixty days, he was told. Rusty was in the same boat. The police had searched Dunningham's office at Wits but came up with nothing incriminating.

Glenn was in grade four at Saint John's and no longer wanted to be a cowboy. He wanted to be an astronaut. A bright boy, a good soccer player and cricketer, he did his homework, didn't get in trouble. His report cards were good; the teachers liked him. It didn't seem to matter that he was Jewish at an Anglican school. His only complaint was that his teacher wouldn't let them eat cake for Pete Blagden's birthday, even though the boy's mother made it herself and brought enough for everyone.

Sarah had been struggling to get pregnant again. They hadn't had sex very much lately—Henry said he was too tense. Still, they went to her gynaecologist, a kindly, patrician man who nodded when he spoke, as if he were agreeing with himself. He ruled out endometriosis and uterine cysts, assured them her reproductive organs were healthy. Not to worry, he said, it would eventually happen. As they walked out of the building, Henry said they should keep trying, and she smiled and kissed him, holding his hand as they walked back to the car.

WINTER. NELLIE and Henry spread a blanket in a patch of pale sunshine at the back of Colin's garden. He brought news, none of it good. The Sabotage Act had been passed, defining terrorism in the broadest of terms and allowing for ninety-day detention without trial. The very next day, they'd arrested Sisulu.

"So, Walter is gone," she said quietly.

"For the time being, yes."

When she looked at Henry he touched her shoulder, and she put her hand on his. He pulled her hand to his chest, and spread her fingers across his shirt. He leaned forward as she turned to face him. And then he kissed her. She tasted sweet, like a nectarine. She smiled, and then they kissed again, more passionately this time. Something was lifting his heart, his quiet restrained heart was light as a cloud—rising, floating.

They pulled apart, looked away for a moment.

"Come here." Her hand, soft as silk on his neck.

And they kissed again.

When they drew apart he could still taste her, but he stood up. He had a six thirty curfew.

AT HOME he felt guilty and awkward, couldn't sit still. Sarah tried to soothe him. He shouted at Glenn. "No radio until you've finished your homework."

Later, in bed, Sarah asked if he thought he could get approval to go on holiday. "It'd do us all good to get away," she said, looking at him intently.

"Glenn has school."

"He can miss a few days."

He said he didn't think the magistrate would grant him leave, but he'd try anyway.

"Everything will be okay," she said. "We just have to be careful."

Her eyes were inquiring and compassionate in equal parts. Her *geshvolen* lips. Was he acting strangely? Of course he was. But she had no way of knowing why, and probably put it down to the stress of house arrest. And she was partly right. He was going mad, taunted by the hidden face of power. Sometimes he was consumed by fear, and sometimes it all felt horribly normal.

Another visit. Henry had abandoned all pretence and did not bother to call on Colin. He found Nellie in the garden, sitting on the fountain perch, reading a paperback. She moved over when he approached, and put the book in her lap. He sat beside her. Above them, a darkening sky roiled; the wind was picking up. He told her the Defense and Aid Fund had just won the acquittal of seventy-eight people charged under the Sabotage Act.

"Ah, that's good news. You see, Henry, some of the time we are winning."

"Yes, some of the time."

A sudden thunderclap, the sky tightened, and then the smell of cool rain on thirsty grass. Nellie laughed and started towards the little cottage, her head down as she ran through the rain. Henry followed, slipping on the slick grass in his Italian shoes.

Inside her room, they stood panting. Beads of water on her face, dripping from her hair. Dark droplets on her face and neck. He ran his fingers up her neck. They drew closer, and he felt her breasts against his chest and pulled her down, kissing her as they teetered, and she let out a laugh as they fell onto the bed, their limbs entwined.

The rain tapped on the drainpipes, *tac-tac-tac*, and he pulled her closer as they kissed, slowly at first, nervous as kids at a school dance. Rain streamed down the window-panes and he lifted her sweater up and over her head.

In August Mandela was arrested. At a roadblock outside Howick, Natal, Mandela disguised as a chauffeur. Police swarmed the car and arrested him. Some said the CIA had tipped off Special Branch. Mandela was supposed to have had dinner with CIA agent Donald Rickard the night of the arrest, so Rickard knew his whereabouts, more or less. From there, the police took Mandela to the Johannesburg Fort, where he was imprisoned.

On Rusty's orders, Henry had only attended one meeting since his house arrest. Now Rusty had also been served banning orders, but with Mandela and Sisulu in prison, they needed to keep things moving. So Henry requested and received permission to see a client in Sandown, drove a circuitous route along a side street, checking his rearview mirror all the while. Only when he was sure he wasn't being followed did he continue on to Liliesleaf.

Inside the cottage, a small group had gathered. Nellie was talking to a young man Henry hadn't met before, and he felt a pang of jealousy. He'd stopped at a bookstore earlier in the week and bought her a collection of poetry and a novel but now felt awkward about giving her the wrapped presents. Dick arrived a few minutes later, and finally Rusty, too, looking harried. Everyone was talking about the arrest.

"Special Branch must have been tipped off."

"But who?"

"The CIA?" It was Rusty who spoke. "An informer, maybe."

Someone said, "We've got to make an escape plan. We must get Nelson out."

They talked about bribing guards, the possibility of a prison break. A general strike was in the works. They needed to keep feeding news to the foreign press.

WITH EACH visit, their lovemaking grew more intense, more ardent, and at the same time more relaxed. Henry was enthralled. He washed in her tiny bathroom with its cold tiled floor, or showered at the university gym on the way home, splashing himself with cologne so that Sarah would not smell another woman on him.

He confessed to Dick, who in turn made his own disclosures. He'd had a tryst with a student, and more recently there'd been a married woman, Mariana. "Just be careful, Hen. Don't want the wife finding out. Get out before things get heavy." But that's exactly what it was—heavy. He didn't say the word to his friend but it flitted through his mind: love. Yes, you could love two women at the same time. Of course, his infidelity could just be a sudden burst of madness, or the illicit action of a man whose every action was illicit, or an act of freedom by a man and woman who were not free. Madness, freedom, doomed love—whatever it was and whatever its impetus, he yearned for his afternoons with Nellie.

NELSON MANDELA'S trial was held in a makeshift courtroom at the Old Synagogue in Pretoria; the large room was full of people, black and white, foreign reporters, friends, family, lawyers. Mandela entered the court wearing a *kaross* made from the skins of jackals, with beads around his neck and ankles. He had been accused of inciting people to strike illegally and of leaving the country without a passport. He conducted his own defence, pleaded not guilty. "I consider myself neither morally nor legally bound to obey laws made by a

Parliament in which I have no representation," he declared. When the judge asked if he had anything further to say, Mandela answered, "Your worship, if I had something more to say I would have said it." There was a ripple of laughter in the courtroom.

Mandela was sentenced to five years in prison. The crowd ignored the prohibition on demonstrations and surged through the streets, singing. *Shosholoza Shosholoza Mandela. Stimela siqabel' eMzantsi-Afrika.* Go forward, Mandela. The train is crossing South Africa.

23. HOSTAGE

The pea-coloured Toyota entered town past a sprawling hospital and a used-car lot. Images flashed through Saul's mind—the barrel of a gun, staring at his own blood, his flesh ripped and gouged. What did it feel like to get shot? Did the pain last very long, or did you go numb? He thought about PlayStation, bang-bang-bang sharpshooting on *Medal of Honour*. People died every day, all the time; people got killed, people who shouldn't get killed. He remembered walking in Lithuania with his grandfather, their trip to Ponar. They'd trudged through thick trees and snow, then arrived at a clearing. A creepy place of hard cold ground and grey sky. Nothing there, just the absence of trees, an ominous hush, and a small stone monument, stark and forlorn. They'd walked around the circular patches of grass ringed by low walls. This was where the Jews were killed and left in huge pits. Henry's uncles and aunts and cousins had died right there. So had thousands of others, one hundred thousand souls. The guide told them that once in a while, someone would survive, a child usually, missed by a bullet and breathing in a pit of warm corpses, and after lying there for a while, the child would go back to the ghetto and tell what had happened. The image came to him of a girl running through a snowy forest, blood-spattered and terrified, running away from hell. No one chooses death, he realised; it chooses you.

They pulled up at an outdoor market—stalls selling fruit and vegetables and discount beauty products. A row of painted clay guinea fowl, blue and shiny, stood beside some Chinese tin toys; the next stall sold gourds and kalimbas. And an ATM. Not Nedbank, but FNB, with an illuminated sign—an umbrella-shaped tree against a vivid orange sky. Saul knew then that he wasn't going to make a run for it, wasn't going to scream or try to overpower a man with a gun. His only choice was whether to take out a wad of cash at the ATM or go along with Vusi's plan to get the Nelspruit pirates to the Nedbank. His mind was buzzy and jangled as Sipho stopped the engine and Fat Man told him to get out.

"Okay. Slowly. You don't run, you don't shout, you don't look at anybody. Understand?"

He tasted reflux. "Yes." The irritation in his voice surprised him.

An arm snaked around the seat back, dropped his ATM card in his lap.

Saul reached for the door handle, but the big guy put his hand on the door.

"I'm right behind you."

"I understand." He hated the guy. Fat bastard. Dickhead. He wanted him dead, expunged, removed from the planet. Preferably painfully. Wanted him to suffer.

"It's First National Bank," he said. His voice sounded tinny, distant. "FNB won't work. Didn't in Johannesburg."

"What? Rubbish. Go."

"I'm telling you."

He unlocked his door, opened it slowly. He heard the back door open and close. He walked the few feet to the ATM machine on jelly legs, a whistling sound in his ears. Fat Man was so close that Saul could smell the onions on his breath. Stay calm, he told himself.

He inserted his card and keyed in the code, getting one number wrong. Beep-beep-beep-beep. 5221 instead of 5224. An alert message appeared. Please re-enter your password. Same wrong number, same error message.

Fat Jack was peering around his shoulder now, looking at the screen.

"I told you. It's a Cirrus card. Bank of America. Only works with Nedbank machines in South Africa. There's nothing I can do."

"Back in the car."

There was a hand on his shoulder, and he was prodded back inside the car.

As Sipho started the ignition, Saul felt Fat Man's eyes on him. Maybe he was weighing up the situation; maybe he was deciding what to do with him after they robbed him. Kill him? Take him back to his hotel?

"*Masihambe*," he said to Sipho, slapping his seat back. "Nedbank."

24. HENRY AGONISTES

Henry wasn't there. That crackly cold day in July 1963. Mandela wasn't there either; he was already in jail. Orange was back in Natal. Ravi was dead. Slovo was in exile. So were Tambo and Kotane. Luthuli was on the run. Dunningham was lecturing. A laundry van pulled up outside Liliesleaf. The doors flew open, and police jumped out, weapons drawn as they ran through the property, shouting, "Don't move! Stay where you are!" More police cars pulled through the gates, and officers with dogs circled the grounds. The high priests were cuffed and shunted into police vans. Nowhere to hide. Plainclothes policemen took their time searching for evidence. When the dogs stopped barking an eerie stillness came over the place. They found files, notebooks, papers—hauled it all off in cardboard boxes.

Henry read the news that evening in a note from Hilda, sent via a supermarket delivery boy. He sat in the study with the lights off, looking at the dark shapes of trees.

"What is it, Hen? What's wrong?" Sarah in the doorway.

"Rusty didn't come home. Hilda thinks he's been arrested."

She came up behind him and wrapped her arms around him.

"He was at Liliesleaf."

"Oh, God. No. You can't stay here."

Later that evening, Janey knocked on the study door. "Someone in the kitchen to see you."

"In the kitchen?"

"Yes."

There in the kitchen stood Nellie, dressed like a domestic. Her eyes looked strained, as if she'd been crying.

"It's bad," she said quietly. "They got everyone. Not just that. They also got papers, plans, names, addresses—a lot of documents."

"Prosecutor's treasure trove," Henry said. "How did they manage to infiltrate? Or did someone turn?"

She shook her head.

A burst of panic. Were the cops on their way to arrest him? He squeezed her hands briefly, then they drew apart, alone with shared fear.

"I have to go now," she said. "I have to disappear."

"Where will you go?"

"A township, probably Jabulani. For now, at least. It's safer."

"Is Zeke . . . ?"

"Zeke is in Lobatse. He's safe." And then, "I'm not going there." A confession? Lover to lover? Or some sort of rebuke? He couldn't tell.

"Won't you stay? Something to eat?"

"I can't. No time."

He wanted to be far away, somewhere else, with her. He wanted to hold her in the moonlight, to sleep entwined, and couldn't imagine being away from her, not knowing where she was. A speckled blue pot stood on the draining board beside the sink. He'd never noticed it before. He wondered how many more times he would eat in this kitchen, how many more nights he would spend in his home, and when he'd see Nellie again. Everything was shattering, scattering, and he felt a rush of terror even as he struggled to comprehend what was going on around them.

"You've got to go too. Fast as you can. They've got all the papers, everything. Soon they're going to have our names. It's just a matter of time."

"I know," he said.

"They'll try to arrest everybody."

"I know."

One way or another, they were going to take away everything he loved. They looked at each other. Nellie's lips quivered; she was on the verge of tears. She held his hand for a minute, then turned and let herself out of the kitchen door. She crossed the cement courtyard and opened the back door. She didn't turn around. The last he saw of her was her silhouette in the doorway.

HENRY PHONED Dunningham.

"Hello, Henry old boy. Just thinking about you."

Henry could hear from his voice that Dick had already heard and was in a panic, even as he tried to sound nonchalant.

"Sarah wants to know if you and Daisy can come for supper on Saturday."

"Saturday? Terribly sorry. I've got a conference this weekend."

He'd seen Dunningham two days before. Conference meant he was on the run. Henry pictured him packing his pigskin suitcase, rushing around the house.

"How are you feeling? Has the doctor been round?"

"No, I'm okay. No doctor visits."

Escape routes were in place, plans ready. But this wasn't what anyone had predicted. They thought there might be a leak, an arrest or two, but nothing like this. This was everyone, every damned document. They had it all now.

He found Sarah upstairs. "Dick's running," he told her.

"I phoned my parents. They're expecting us. We'd better get a move on."

And they swept into action. Henry filled a suitcase with toothbrush and a change of clothes. He packed quickly, knowing that he was forgetting things, wondering all the while whether there'd be a knock on the door and it would be too late to run, too late to flee, too late to do anything but go to jail.

He tiptoed into Glenn's room, sat on the edge of the boy's bed and watched him sleep for a while, then kissed him and hugged him as hard as he could without waking him.

Sarah drove. Henry lay on the backseat of the car, watching treetops and lampposts whirl by. When they arrived, she got out first. Returned with her father, in his dressing gown and slippers, an arm around his daughter. He flashed Henry a look of reproach—*How dare you endanger my daughter*! They whisked him into the room above the garage, where they made up an old mattress. Aniela and Sarah brought in a fan and radio and some old magazines and books. Meyer had said he could stay in the guest room, but they both said no. It was too risky. This way her parents could deny that they knew he was there. If the police visited them, there would be nothing to hide.

Sarah stayed with him late that first night. He was afraid, but there was nothing else they could do at that moment.

"It's up to you," he said. "I'll stay if you want to stay."

"Of course I want to stay, Hen. Don't you? Our life is here, our families, everything. But not if it means that you go to jail. Of course not."

"Mandela's ready to die for freedom."

"Well, I'm not."

He wasn't either. The thought of arrest, trial, prison filled him with a helpless, consuming terror. "But we have to be prepared for the worst, and know that it's a possibility. They could find me. I'm not safe yet."

"Don't talk rubbish. You're not going on trial for treason." Sarah, the philosopher, the logician, was calm. "We have the whole world to be free in."

Hazel Simmons was someone they could reach out to. She would know how to get them out. A man called Boshoff sold fake passports. It would cost money, of course. They had some cash stashed in the back of a desk drawer. For a rainy day. It was a rainy day.

THEY CAME the next day. Two patrol cars. The two men who came to the door were polite, gracious even, both in plain-clothes, suits and white shirts. The officer's name was Baylor. English-speaking, handsome. He apologised for bothering her. Where was Mr. Wegland? He hadn't checked in at the police station, which was a violation of the magistrate's orders.

She said he was in Pretoria at a mining conference. Didn't know the hotel. They could check with his secretary.

The cop gave a thin smile. Handed her his card. "Please call us if you hear from him, okay? Or if he comes back."

HENRY STAYED in the room above the garage, huddled and nervous. Smoking (even though he'd never been much of a smoker), reading the newspaper and old magazines. His heart raced every time he heard a car in the driveway. He learned the sound of Meyer's Mercedes and Aniela's Opel. He played the radio, softly, used the servants' toilet, didn't switch on the light after dark. The room was cold at night. There was a little electric heater, but it didn't do very much except make noise.

After Liliesleaf, more arrests soon followed. Goldreich, Wolpe, Denis Goldberg. MK was in tatters, its leadership dec-imated. The Liliesleaf gardener—Mpilo—had disappeared. Luthuli, mysteriously, had eluded capture. Everyone who hadn't been arrested was in hiding. Escape plans were in motion. Chaos ensued, as rumours spread among the scared and running and incredulous.

How had it come to this? The others were in prison. They would be charged with treason, and if they were found guilty they would be hanged or spend the rest of their lives behind bars.

Was Special Branch closing in on him, even as he sat there, face to the window, staring at the wattle trees and swimming pool? *Avadim hayinu, ata b'nei chorin.* It was almost funny, his rattled mind going back to Passover with his parents, prayers for freedom.

In the dark expanse of night, anything could sound like a van in the driveway, footsteps on the slate path.

"You'll be fine. No one knows you're here," Sarah tried to reassure him.

They sat on the mattress, side by side.

"We don't know that for sure."

She stroked his stubble and kissed the top of his cheek lightly. "We do. We do know that. They're so happy with the arrests, they're not worrying about you. They got the big fish. Now the little fish can swim away."

The newspapers were full of the news. The Liliesleaf nine were in detention. They would go on trial. Rumour had it the state would seek the death penalty. But that hadn't been confirmed.

Sarah had contacted Hazel Simmons. If anyone could organise an escape, Hazel could. She had a whole network of ANC operatives, people who provided shelter, forgers, drivers. Right now, her network was in motion—a house was being set up, escape routes figured out. She was in touch with Daisy Dunningham. Dick was hiding out at a friend of his cousin's, somewhere the police wouldn't look. Hazel sent a note to Sarah with the greengrocer's deliveries: *Now would be a good time for H. to leave. Meet D. at a safe house in Rhodesia. Plane to Lagos. Everything arranged. Get foreign currency. Destroy this note.*

IN CASE she'd been followed, Sarah ate dinner with her parents before preparing a plate of food and slipping out to the garage. Henry listened as she told him about Hazel's plan.

"When?"

"Soon. She'll let us know."

She poured him a glass of wine and watched him eat.

"It's going to be cold in America," she said. "But you'll eat cheesecake and a New York steak. You'll see Bob and Gail."

They'd talked about London. Henry didn't want to go to England; Sarah didn't either. God knows, his father would prefer America. Jakub had worked at a Ford dealership for many years and knew people in Detroit and Dearborn, cities somewhere in the middle of the country. He loved America the way he had once loved South Africa, the way you could only love an idea, not a real country.

"Did you talk to Boschoff about the passport?"

"Yes. All taken care of. You just have to be patient."

"Not so easy," he said and tried to smile. "To be a patient little fish." If he was arrested he didn't want Sarah to be there, in case he broke down or pissed himself. He didn't want to have to be brave for anyone else.

HE SPENT two days leafing through back copies of *Vogue* and *Time* and trying to read a John O'Hara novel. But he couldn't concentrate. He wanted to see his boy, wanted to touch him, smell him, hear him laugh. Sarah had told him that Henry had been called away suddenly on business. Meyer delivered Henry's supper on a plate covered with aluminum foil. There was only one chair, and although Henry offered, insisted, Meyer didn't sit down. He was stiff and formal, as Henry imagined he might behave towards a new silversmith in the back room of his shop, not exactly throwing his weight around, but making sure the man knew he was rigorous, tough. For his part, Henry felt like an impecunious immigrant, begging for work or alms. Meyer was angry at him, but was he angry at Sarah as well? Maybe. But clearly he held Henry to blame. They never discussed any of this, only the food, the weather, and did he need anything. No, Henry assured him, once again, and thanked him.

"Please thank Nela for supper."

He ate a little, but he wasn't hungry. He covered the plate with the foil and put it beside the door, and he sat on the bed and stared at the wall, at the patch of sky outside the window and the beige electric heater.

There was a lot of time to think. About Nellie, about Sarah, about things he thought he'd forgotten. Like Harry Houdini, his childhood hero. The postcard Isaac had given him—Houdini enmeshed in a dozen locks and chains. Where was Nellie now? Was she with Zeke? Hiding in plain view in Jabulani or Alex?

He remembered leaving Liverpool, aboard the *HMS Arundel Castle*, its soaring iron decks coated in paint so thick you could press your fingernail in it and leave a crescent moon, remembered the loud horn as tugs pulled the ship out of the harbour, waves slapping its massive hull, and then the open sea, the great green swell of the Atlantic surging around them.

"We're going, boys," Jakub had said, gazing at the horizon and narrowing his eyes, as if he could finally apprehend the contours of the future. "To the prize of an empire."

"Don't get lost. No running." His mother's imprecations trailed off as Henry ran from their cabin in his scratchy wool suit and went to explore the upper deck, tiptoeing past the first-class cabins, where men played cards and ladies walked with parasols, and servants trailed like shadows, carrying books and cotton blankets or wheeling infants in ornate prams. He liked watching the crew, the sailors with their beards and big hands. He enjoyed standing on the deck, feeling the rise and fall of the ship as it sluiced through powerful swells, ploughing through an ocean that seemed to go on and on forever. Sometimes there was another ship, a dark blob on the horizon, sometimes the sea was calm as glass, and sometimes it was furrowed as if the bottom of the ocean was churning, sending huge spasms of waves upwards to the sky.

Henry looked after his little brother, held his hand and walked with him. "Come, Mikey." And little Mikey would take his hand and walk beside him, one slow two-year-old step at a time, across the deck, where they could watch the crew and gaze at the horizon, at the green below and the blue above.

THEY MOVED him again, this time in the back of a carpenter's van. To the Murrays' house in Woodmead. Hazel had made the arrangements. Friends of the movement, no one he or Sarah knew. An unused servant's room at the bottom of the garden, eight meters square, a concrete box with a single window and a padlocked door, though Henry could easily reach through the window and open the lock. A mattress on the floor, a sheet draped across the window, a jug of water and a glass.

It was usually Astrid, young, wide-eyed, invariably wearing a kaftan, who brought him a sandwich and tea in a thermos. Over the next few days, he was twice invited up to the house for a shower and some supper. They didn't talk much; Henry was polite, solemn. It was a kind of jail. Like any prisoner, his job was to wait now, to do nothing, to read whatever was available in his cell, piss in the bushes, to endure. Immigrant, emigrant, refugee. The words rattled around in his mind. On the deck of the *Arundel Castle*, he'd imagined that the horizon was the edge of the world. Immigrant, emigrant, refugee, pissing in the bushes.

HE FOUGHT the urge to run, even as he sat reading a dog-eared copy of Hammond Innes's *The White South*. He tried to imagine New York, saw the city as a series of images like the ones on Glenn's View-Master, where you saw a three-dimensional picture, clicked the lever, saw another. Airport, the Chrysler Building, Central Park. He felt like he was in a dark tunnel, crawling slowly to freedom. Would his captors be waiting at the other end? Was he walking into a trap? How proud his father had been aboard the *Arundel* in his woollen suit, staring intently at the sea as if divining their future in the icy waves. Their first port of call was Madeira. In six days they'd be there, his father had said, in Africa. Henry could not get the image of a jungle out of his mind, although his father had told him there were big cities, that it was an advanced country—"prosperous" was the word he used—and his eyes had shone with an intensity as if the word, the place, was full of magic. Henry's mind spun with pictures of lions roaming the streets of a city with majestic buildings like Liverpool's Canning Place and Scotland Road. But also, he'd felt the vague pang of everything left behind, his entire life, lost in the ship's wake, like a dream that dissolves—Uncle Isaac, Lime Street, the smell of hair oil and leather outside the hairdresser's, the picture of Jack Johnson he'd cut out of the newspaper, towering above his opponent, head thrust forward like a bull, gloves raised high above his head. Inhaling the briny smell of the sea, he gazed at the numinous horizon, the water crested with tails of white under a grey Atlantic sky. In the cabin at night, Mama sang to Mikey. *"Shlof, mayn kind, mayn treyst, mayn sheyner."* Sleep, my child, my comfort, my beauty.

Henry asked what language they spoke in Africa. "English, of course," his father snorted. There was a map in one of the staterooms, where Jakub showed him their route. Henry imagined their ship sailing around the jagged chunks of continents, a dot slithering down the shiny paper sea, all the way to the bottom of Africa, the bottom of the world. Jakub pointed, and Henry could see the zeal in his eyes. "You boys will go to a good school. You will be educated gentlemen." And he shook his big hand as if dusting a cobweb in the air above the great, gilded Atlantic crisscrossed with lines of latitude and longitude—clearing away all the nameless, ugly things they were leaving behind.

One night, Jakub and Henry went walking on the deck. Stars glimmered above veils of clouds; the ship's lights cast a yellow glow on the dark water. They heard music up above, the muffled sounds of violins and cellos tumbling downward.

"Come on," Jakub said, and Henry took his hand and they made their way up the steps to the first-class hall. The music grew louder, and through the steamy windows they saw a quintet playing, the musicians in black ties and crisp white shirts, the passengers draped in pearls and gold. And now Henry could hear the music clearly, the moan of an oboe rising above the strings, and he tugged his father's shirt and whispered in his ear. "They're playing Bach."

"Yes? How do you know?"

"Uncle Isaac used to sing it with me . . . On his coal runs."

"Coal runs," his father said, and something about the intonation hinted at his disbelief. "You know the story about your great-uncle, Zalman Beker," his father said, as they made their way back to their cabin.

Though Henry knew the story, he said, "Tell me, Papa."

"Well, your Great-Uncle Zalman was a marvellous musician. When he played the cello ladies would burst out crying, it was so beautiful. Around this time, there was a lot of persecution. The Russians overran villages, and when you saw them coming you fled, otherwise you'd face possible death. Well, when they came to the town of Valmiera, where Zalman was visiting with a popular quartet, he didn't get any warning. And when the Russians came, he was asleep in his room above the music hall.

"He had no time to gather his things, so he ran, dressed only in his undergarments and coat, clutching his cello. He could hear the shooting and fighting at the edge of town, and so he kept running, the sound of horses and screaming behind him. He ran out of the town's gates with his cello, and kept running until he reached the river. And as the Russians came closer he stepped into the cold river and set sail on his cello. He held on to the floating cello case, his coat trailing behind him, and escaped. They say he travelled for miles down the Gauja River, all the way to Cesis, and after some time, he came back to his family in Lithuania."

Two days later, a Tuesday, Sarah arrived with news. He was about to spend his fourth night in the concrete box.

"Everything is ready. Hazel says tomorrow morning. Seven o'clock, be at the bus stop on Jan Smuts. There's a house in Gibeon—it's a town in Rhodesia. From there you'll get to Salisbury."

She'd brought clean underpants and two shirts in a shopping bag. He noticed a small photograph at the bottom of the bag, in a silver frame. The three of them at the Vaal River, in the sun. He'd add it to the one he'd taken. Two photographs and a change of clothes. Not much for a man leaving his life behind.

A red travel agent's pouch contained two passports, his real one and a forged one, as well as a wad of cash, all neatly organised. Another bag contained his disguise. When he looked through the contents, he couldn't help smiling.

"Whose idea was that?"

"I don't know. Hazel's, I suppose."

They made love on the single mattress surrounded by empty cans of peaches and peas, a scatter of magazines and books. Afterwards, he lay back on the bed and watched her pull on her pantyhose. Her legs were gorgeous to him then. Her shoulder blades rippled under her auburn hair. He wanted to lay his head in her mussed hair and stay there.

"There's one more thing," she said. She was dressed now, sitting apart from him, on the edge of the mattress. "You won't ever, ever sleep with another woman. Not here, not there."

"I . . ." He looked at her, at the accusation in her eyes.

Nearby, a radio was playing softly. Folk music wafted through the open window.

"I love you," he said.

She sighed, pulled at her fingers.

"I'm so sorry." He didn't know what to say. How had she found out, and why had she waited until now to confront him?

"And she's black. Christ, Henry. What will people say?"

"I don't think the colour of her skin is the point." He had to fight to control his rising anger.

But she was angry too, staring at him with steely eyes. "It's the point if I say it is. What? Were you trying to prove something?"

"No."

"Embarrass me?"

"I'm sorry."

Hurt and blame in her eyes—also an animal softness.

She let him take her hand, and they sat without speaking, holding hands like teenagers at the cinema.

"I love you," he said again.

She let him touch her face, kiss the soft skin of her neck. He didn't want to let her go, and held on to her hand as she stood up. She slipped on her shoes and picked up her handbag. He rose too, hugged her. He wanted her to stay, but he was also frightened, and wanted to be alone with his fear, to stop pretending he was brave.

"Be careful," she said.

"I will, of course. Give Glenn a hug from me."

She let herself out. He listened to the clap of her shoes on the pathway outside. A minute later, the sound of her car reversing down the driveway.

It was barely dawn when he shaved, slathered foundation over his chin, stuffed his passport and a wad of US dollars into his underpants, and then dressed himself in the prickly polyester nun's habit and veil. At six thirty, he walked to the bus stop on Jan Smuts Avenue. Waited in the morning sun. A dented brown Datsun stopped, and a man he'd never seen before leaned across the passenger seat.

"Sister, can I give you a lift?"

He tossed his bags onto the backseat. And then he was bouncing along the Johannesburg streets. The battered handbag on his lap contained a rosary, a handkerchief, a small purse, and the passport of Sister Mary O'Donoghue.

The car took him all the way to Pietersburg. They didn't talk much. Henry said thank you, and the driver, who never told Henry his name, replied that it was nothing, the least he could do. When he dropped Henry in Pietersburg he gave him a note with directions and an address. "Go safely. Good luck."

At the bus station, Henry bought a ticket for Rutenga. Waited in the winter sun, sweating in the dark nun's habit. *A little onward lend thy guiding hand to these dark steps.*

THE BUS smelled of sweat and vinyl. No one seemed to notice him, and yet he felt observed. He couldn't shake the fear that today would be the last day of his life, that he would be discovered, hauled off the bus, shot in the back of the head, left in a ditch at the side of the road. Or imprisoned for sedition, treason, crimes against the state. He closed his eyes and whispered a silent prayer, and then laughed at himself, the atheist Jew dressed as a nun praying to a God who seemed not to favour the Struggle.

They stopped at a petrol station in Louis Trichardt, trundled past low, white farmhouses with red-tiled roofs, acacia trees, and thorny scrub, drove through the Soutpansberg, through Messina to the Limpopo River. At Beit Bridge, the border police boarded the bus, but none looked closely at the tired, ugly nun hugging her bag. His thighs and balls were sweating onto the plastic bag that contained US dollars and his real passport. He didn't make eye contact, just handed over his nun's passport, then clasped his fingers to hide the hair on his hand, and returned to his rosary beads. Then the bus was moving again, and they crossed Beit Bridge into Rhodesia, Henry thinking, I'm out, thinking, the nun is a Jewish man, and he's slipping through your hands.

In Rhodesia the road narrowed, and few cars sped by. They passed vast, empty *veld*, low trees, stone *rondavels* with thatched roofs, mud shacks, herds of impala, and the odd lone duiker. Bright-green birds skimmed the treetops. When they arrived in Rutenga, it was already late and the bus was almost empty. He had slipped through locks and chains and borders. Like Henry Houdini. Like his Great-Uncle Zalman, who had eluded the Cossack cavalry, armed only with a cello and *chutzpah*.

An old man in a wheezing car gave him a lift to Gibeon. Empty countryside, telephone poles, spindly trees, scrub. Snippets of his father's story about Zalman drifted through his mind: the man from Jonava who had travelled for a while with musical troupes until the war came and all the Jews of Jonava were killed or sent to Stutthof camp. None of Zalman's family had survived.

They had read about the Lithuanian Activist Front, knew about the Nazi occupation and the Blitz. In Liverpool, children and mothers had been evacuated. Saint Luke's destroyed, the Overhead Railway bombed, Wapping Dock and Upper Stanhope Street, too. Nearly two thousand dead in Merseyside in a single month in 1941. The newsreels showed a city dark and decimated, buildings smashed and ugly, stone and iron like grotesque bones splayed in rubble—grey, broken. "What if the Germans bomb here?" Henry had asked his father. "Don't be stupid," Jakub replied. "The war is not here. We're safe." Africa seemed a much better place to be.

And while Europe lay smoldering and ravaged, a ruddy-faced Port Elizabeth businessman named Smythe who had close ties to Detroit offered Jakub the job of managing a new Ford dealership in Johannesburg, and so, once again, he packed up his family and left for a better life. They bought a bigger house with a proper garden; Eva planted rose bushes and yellow daisies. At her urging, they joined the Ponevez Synagogue in Doornfontein and contributed money and clothing to a relief fund for Lithuanian *landsleit*. In the evenings,

Henry sat with his father and brother in the big carpeted living room in their new house, listening to the SABC and the BBC on Jakub's shortwave radio. They learned about the Blitz, about the Luftwaffe and firestorms and bomb shelters. E. M. Forster hosted a programme after the news once a week, discussing Wordsworth and Trilling, Matthew Arnold and the Renaissance. On one of his shows, sometime in 1943, Forster said something that Henry never forgot: "In the catastrophe that has befallen our civilisation, we have all become callous as an alternative to insanity."

GIBEON WAS little more than a crossroads. A few shops, a small church, open stalls selling farm produce. Sister Mary gave the driver a banknote, then walked off stiffly, carrying her BOAC bag and suitcase to the general store where she asked to use the phone.

25. KELP

A gust of cold air and street sounds accompanied Glenn as he walked in the front door. He called hello, and Henry in the living room called hello back.

"Dad, how do you feel? Let's take a look at you."

"I'm fine. Just a bit banged up."

He watched as Glenn stowed his briefcase at the foot of the stairs.

Holly appeared from the kitchen and gave Glenn a kiss. "He wouldn't let me take him to the emergency room."

Henry knew from her tone that she hadn't said anything to Glenn about what he'd witnessed earlier.

"She tried," he said. "Badgered me for hours. Anyway, I'm fine, really. How was your day? Good drink with that client?"

"Potential client. Unlikely client. He's not building a new restaurant, not now, anyway. I doubt he's got the funding, just wants to talk about his dream."

HOLLY COOKED salmon with fresh ginger, and they talked about a new play at the Harvey Theater. Henry's arse and side hurt. He squirmed in his chair. Despite the pills and scotch, he couldn't elude the pain, which snaked inside him. He sensed he'd have trouble walking tomorrow. They talked about what Saul was doing. Holly liked the idea of his applying for a grant to make a documentary about South Africa, but Glenn thought it sounded like a long shot—he should rather concentrate on his studies and land an internship that would look good on his résumé.

Holly and Glenn spoke about weekend plans with friends in the neighbourhood, Henry watched them, scanning for signs of trouble. If there were any, he couldn't detect them. Then again, there were certain things that were invisible, even to a father or father-in-law. Best not to worry about everyone else's cards. It was up to Holly; she would decide what happened next. He didn't want to meddle. When he looked up, Holly was watching him with her cat's eyes.

After they'd washed up and Holly had put leftovers in Tupperware containers, she went upstairs to take a bath. Glenn and Henry sat at the table and finished their wine.

"I talked to that lawyer today," Glenn said.

"And?"

"Not good."

Glenn repeated what the lawyer had told him: because Henry didn't actually live in the Red Hook building—even though he'd designated it his primary residence for tax purposes—it wasn't a property they wanted to subject to a lot of scrutiny. Worse, although the mortgage was underwater, they weren't eligible for the Homeowner Affordability and Stability Plan, because of the qualification requirements.

"So what do we do?"

"Nothing we can do. Just wait. Wait until a bank gives you a better mortgage, until people start to pay higher rents in Red Hook again, or we get a decent offer. Until then, we're underwater. We're kelp."

Henry pictured the building underwater, awash in seaweed, schools of fish darting in and out of the windows, squid on the roof. It wasn't just the house. The stocks Henry had squirrelled away, Saul's college fund, Henry's retirement fund—it was all underwater. All his life, investments had gone up, property values had risen, and now, suddenly, the world was in reverse. It had happened with ferocious speed, caught him unawares.

Glenn had drawn up beautiful plans to renovate the Red Hook building, extend the garden, build a deck, put in skylights, redo the bathrooms and kitchens. He'd unfurled the plans for Henry and gone through them, pointing here and there to explain how the outside stairs would look and where he would punch out big windows in the back. He'd even described the tiles and glass bricks he had in mind for the bathrooms.

"You drew up such beautiful plans," Henry said.

"Thanks, Dad. That and three dollars will buy you a latte."

Glenn sounded okay, but looked so disconsolate now, hunched over at the table, swirling the wine in his glass. Henry didn't know what to say. Don't be so gloom and doom? Actually, your wife's also having an affair, in case you didn't know? No, none of that would do.

Glenn's dream was dissolving, the dream of starting his own firm, of buying and converting Brooklyn buildings. And Henry's dream too, the dream of making his son's dreams come true. He wished there were more—more money, more sources of income, more houses, more time. Henry looked at Glenn and recalled a recurrent dream. In it, a man stood alone on a deserted island, not a beautiful island but one with a gummy beach and abandoned buildings and rusting metal, an island of detritus and muck. Sometimes it was Glenn alone on the sand; and sometimes it was Henry.

26. ON FERREIRA STREET

Saul squeezed his knees together and let his head go slack against the seat back. Saul Lionel Wegland, twenty years old, he thought. Found dead in a ditch near Nelspruit, South Africa. A memorial service will be held. The funeral will be. Saul was best known for. What? There was no brilliant documentary, no achievements whatsoever. He barely had a past. He was all future. And more than anything, he wanted that future.

They were in the city centre now, on Ferreira Street. Colourful shops, palms and flame trees, streetlights and pedestrians flashed past. A mother and child, a shirtless man driving an old car. For everyone else, it was just a normal day. He sensed that he wasn't dealing with seasoned criminals—these guys were amateurs. Maybe they were friends of Sipho's. Maybe they'd followed them from the lodge. Sipho could have tipped them off. They had a gun, but that didn't make them killers. I can survive this, he thought.

Fat Man spoke and they slowed down. Saul saw the big Nedbank sign, the electric doors. The building itself was made of pale brick and glass. It looked like the main branch.

Sipho pulled up in a parking spot with a yellow wheelchair sign.

"Okay, let's go."

Saul hated the fat fuck. But he opened the door, climbed out slowly, aware of the gun behind him. A jumble of noises—cars, hooting, his own rushed breathing.

He stood at the ATM machine and drew his bank card from his pocket. He told himself that soon he'd be ordering room service in his Johannesburg hotel, but he wasn't sure he believed it, and a fresh wave of panic surged through him as he stood there, frozen.

A Cadbury's wrapper lay on the cement at his feet. A woman stood behind them, blotchy skin, stringy hair, and bad makeup. He inserted the ATM card. His hands were trembling as he keyed in the number. The machine beeped and the screen changed. *Withdrawal. Deposit. Account Enquiry.*

He touched the withdrawal icon. *Ping.*

Four thousand rand was the maximum amount. Five hundred dollars or so. Ping.

There was an animation of a hand, and banknotes, green and black, pixelated. Discount bobo ATMs they had here in Africa, he thought, as the machine spat out the notes.

Saul pulled the bills from the machine's mouth and shoved them in his pocket. There were a lot of them, and they formed a bulge in his pocket. When he turned, the fat guy nodded.

"Again."

He inserted his card again, keyed in his code, pressed the withdrawal button. *Ping.* The machine whirred.

Again the machine spat out a clump of brown two-hundred-rand notes. Again he shoved them in his pocket. It was done, he thought. No cavalry in sight. He pondered whether he should make a run for it now, toss the bills into the air and escape into the noisy crowd.

When he turned around, his captor was smiling, looking at Saul and his bulging pocket. He wasn't looking behind him, and Saul tried to hide the flicker in his eyes when he saw three men converge behind Fat Man. The stringy-haired woman saw them too, and stepped aside. The three guys fanned out, and Saul backed away. He saw that a fourth guy was standing next to the car, his hand clasping Sipho's neck. The cavalry had arrived.

A second later, Fat Man sensed that something was going on, and he turned around. One of them pounced, shoving him back towards the parking lot. He stumbled. *"Haikona."*

The guy yanked him by his shirt, while his two accomplices came up from behind and grabbed Fat Man's arms, locking them behind his back. Saul ducked behind a car—if the guy shot anyone, it would probably be him. The guy holding Fat Man's shirt smiled, just for an instant, then swung hard. The blow landed squarely on his jaw and sent him spinning back into the other two, who took his gun and kept his arms pinned behind him. The stringy-haired woman took off down the street as the guy punched him again, once in the mouth, twice in the kidneys. There was blood on his mouth, dark and red and syrupy, dripping across his teeth and down his lips. A few drops splattered onto his green shirt.

Tentatively, Saul emerged from behind the parked car.

The boxer turned to him. "I hope you are Vusi's friend."

"Yes. I'm Saul." He felt like singing. Or fainting.

The other two guys pushed their victim towards a waiting car. Sipho's car door opened, and he was hauled out and shoved onto the backseat. A moment later, both cars roared off.

The boxer shook Saul's hand, then clenched and unclenched his fist. He rubbed a hand across his shaved head. "My name is Bongani Mkhwanazi. But everyone calls me Bonga. I'm sorry for what happened to you, but it's okay now."

"Thank you." Saul's legs had gone weak, and he steadied himself against a car. He touched a hand to his pocket. The wad of cash was still there. And he was alive. He wanted to hug Bonga, kiss his shiny pate, jump up and click his heels in the air.

"Come on, come with us." Bonga motioned to some cars parked across the street.

27. Flight

A small house on a lonely, empty road; a rusted green tin roof, old wooden floors. The path outside was marked by rocks, their whitewash faded to a dull grey. *Kishnev*, his mother would have said. As in middle of nowhere. As in *die gramadoelas*. A view of acacia trees and long grass, a dirt road, termite hills. He'd been told the house belonged to a convent. No nuns there now. Nobody but Henry, who waited, smoking, sitting by the window, watching the empty road. Stay inside, they'd told him. There was water in the kitchen, tea, canned fruit.

By now, Sarah would have spoken to his parents. She wouldn't have told them much: Henry is gone; I don't know where he is. The less they knew, the better. His father would be angry, his mother worried and weepy. Such a good son, a good man, how could he do this? Sarah wouldn't tell anyone else. The network had already been compromised.

He sat in front of the open window. A lavender sky dotted with birds, swirls of clouds. Some desiccated insects on the windowsill—paper thin, long dead. There was no fridge, no ice. He was at the edge of the world again, and there was nothing he could do but wait. He drank some lukewarm tap water, and his mind drifted off to that day at the Port Elizabeth dock, with his family in their grey woollen clothes, their scuffed suitcases lined up at the edge of Africa. The small city bursting with colours—green mountainside, bright flowers, crisp white buildings. No ashpits and rot, no tenements. They lived for a few weeks with Herschel and Ethel Rabinowitz, fellow Litvaks, all of them so far away from the world they had left behind forever, and not a rabbi among them to put their souls at ease. Herschel owned a general store on the edge of town. You've done very nicely, Jakub said. My hat to you. His mother took a bracelet from the trunk and held it up to the window, the pink topaz and gold filigree sparkling in the light. Henry didn't know whether she was measuring the light in the new land, or considering its value, or simply looking at it to remember.

H<small>E</small> <small>PISSED</small> on the hot sand outside and stood looking at the flat-topped trees and tattered *veld* with its thorny *dubbeltjies*. He watched as a scorpion scuttled under a rock. If a police van pulled up now there would be no chance of escape, but that knowledge was oddly calming. One day, Herschel arrived in his new car and took Henry and Jakub for a drive around Algoa Bay. Everything was different here—the sun and empty spaces. And the people, the natives whose language sounded like bassoons, the leather-skinned farmers. Even the flies and mosquitoes and bees were nothing like the insects he'd seen before. Afterwards, he stood on the street in front of the Rabinowitzes' house, blinking in the afternoon sunshine, startled by the strange, bright land that was his new home.

He made himself a cup of tea, drank it black, smoked another cigarette. He needed to wash, but the little bathtub was stained and grey and he couldn't be bothered. Waiting had made him indolent.

He tried to sleep, but when he closed his eyes bright flares flickered across the insides of his eyelids, and he jumped at every sound—the creak of floorboards, the shriek of a bird. Where was Sarah? And Nellie? In Jabulani? Back in Breyton?

Dusk. Long shadows, a comic-book crescent moon. And then, out of the hush, came the sound of a car. Henry jumped up and scanned the driveway, watched as a *bakkie* came into view, picking its way along the track. Headlights splashed across the windows. The door opened, and a man got out, clutching a small leather suitcase and a brown shopping bag. Dunningham—hair cut short and dyed black, beard shaven, stood before him.

"Am I pleased to see you," Henry said.

The *bakkie* drove off.

"Can't believe I missed the nun outfit," Dunningham said.

"I did look rather sexy."

They walked inside. Dick dropped his bags on the floor and Henry poured them each a glass of water.

"Everything's collapsed," Dunningham said. "They got everyone."

Henry nodded. Insects buzzed on the *stoep*.

"Well, not everyone."

"Didn't get us."

They clinked glasses.

Dick shook his head slowly. "We're wanted men, though. Not a feeling I like. Hiding. Running."

"Me neither. I thought I was being so careful. Turns out I'm not as good at deception as I thought. "

Dick looked at him, frowned. "You're here, aren't you?"

"I meant Sarah."

"You . . . Sarah knows? About Nellie?"

"Told me the night before I left. She'd been holding on to it for a while."

"Kaboom. I'm sorry. Really bad timing."

Henry stared at his shoes.

Dick turned to survey the little house. Running water and a battery-powered single-coil burner were all the conveniences the house offered. Tin plates beside the kitchen sink, two chipped glasses. A paper shopping bag on the floor contained cigarettes, a couple of cans of spaghetti with meat-balls, Weetabix, condensed milk, instant coffee, sugar.

They smoked cigarettes, spoke about the plan—who'd contact them, what they'd do if the airline tickets failed to materialise. They couldn't stay here forever. They'd hitch, go farther afield. One good piece of news: Dunningham wasn't short of money. All they needed was an airstrip, and he could charter a plane. He had a bag of cash, English pounds and American dollars, and a rich uncle in London.

It was late when they stopped talking and turned off the lights. Henry slept on the couch, covered himself with a musty blanket. He could see the Southern Cross high above the dark land. Moonlight draped itself over the trees. He heard the wind pick up in the middle of the night, leaves whispering, sounds from the hills—cacophonous insects, a lone dog barking.

In the morning they heated water and drank coffee with con-densed milk.

"I need a shave," Henry said.

"Decent meal," Dunningham replied.

"Swim."

"Glass of wine, *blanquette de veau,* peas in butter."

"Steady, now."

Afternoon. Shadows on the grass. Dick lay on his back on the mattress, an arm slung over his eyes. Henry stood up and walked outside, surveying the vast dusty flatness around the house. When he heard the drone of a propeller he rushed inside, but the plane kept moving across the sky, and eventually the sound passed and the black spot vanished from the sky. There weren't many neighbours, but even so, they didn't want to be spotted.

Somewhere, someone was organising their escape. They would send a car. Tickets would be waiting at Salisbury

Airport. And meanwhile, other people were looking for them. They waited for evening, and when they couldn't wait any longer lit a cigarette.

When Dunningham told Henry he'd never left his home before, Henry smiled, "Don't worry, you'll get used to it." It was a *batribt gelegte*, a sad laugh.

THE CAR, a battered Ford Zephyr, appeared the next day. The driver was an old black man who spoke little English, at least to them. They stopped at a garage to piss and buy some bread and cheese, then drove through the Matopo Hills. Rugged scrubby earth around alien boulders. Henry and Dick were grimy and tired and foul-tempered with each other.

At Salisbury Airport they presented their real passports. The fake ones would only pass muster with roadside cops, Hazel had warned them. As the official took his passport, Henry felt his hands go clammy. If his name were on a list, if airport security were cooperating with the South African police to apprehend anyone they took to be a Communist, then he'd be arrested immediately and whisked off to a nearby prison. But nothing like that happened. The heavy-lidded official barely looked up, and loudly stamped his passport.

In the departure lounge they watched the planes taxi and take off. When Dick closed his eyes and pressed his palms together, Henry wondered if he was praying. His own fingers were still trembling slightly.

They boarded the East African Airways Douglas DC-6. No one stopped them. Across the aisle, Dunningham sighed and smiled. The four propellers coughed and came alive. They flew to Nairobi, landing as dawn broke.

At Embakasi Airport they ate eggs with salty cabbage and bacon, then bought two African-style shirts from the airport shop. They sat together in the departure lounge. A workman tended the tarmac outside with a spade and wheelbarrow.

They looked about constantly. Was an undercover agent watching them? Perhaps they'd been followed from the start, Special Branch just having fun, like a cat toying with a mouse. That would be their style, their kind of game. Dunningham told Henry the little he remembered from his one trip to New York—and wrote down the name and address of a friend, an American he'd met at Oxford.

When the flight to London was called, Henry watched Dunningham board, then made his own way to his seat. His heart didn't stop pounding until the plane was airborne. They sat side by side, high above the clouds, each with nothing but a single suitcase and a wad of cash in their hand luggage. Henry ordered a scotch and was somewhat startled by the air hostess who bent over to pour it for him, her clean fresh skin and clear voice. The woman occupying the aisle seat nearest them tried to engage in conversation, and Dunningham obliged, but just for a few minutes. Going home to England, Henry heard him say. Yes, dreadful place, Nairobi. Yes, the mosquitoes. Henry closed his eyes and soon sank into sleep.

The two policemen visited Sarah again. The same polite one, Baylor, asked her where Henry was, did she know where the others were. She said she didn't know what he was talking about. Henry was at a mining conference in Pretoria.

"Come on, Mrs. Wegland. There's no mining conference. Why didn't you file a missing person report?" A coy nod, eyebrows raised, as if it were their little secret, a private joke.

"Because that's what he told me, that he was at a mining conference. He's been gone quite a bit lately. He's . . . seeing someone, another woman." She looked up at him, let him see her shame.

"I see," Baylor said. "I'm sorry, Mrs. Wegland. We have a warrant. We need to search the premises."

"Do you have children, Mr. Baylor?"

"I beg your pardon?"

"Do you have children?"

"Yes."

"Then I'm sure you'll understand. I'm just trying to protect my son. He's just a boy. He hasn't done anything wrong."

Baylor looked her up and down. "Yes, I can understand that. And you have to understand that we don't want to harm you or your boy or search your house. We just want the names and whereabouts of people who have broken the law. You can have your freedom. And the boy's."

"But I don't know anything."

"Then I suggest you find out. You give me some information I can use, and then you can leave, join your husband wherever he is, you and the boy."

"You let my boy leave, and I'll give you some names," she said softly, throatily.

He considered this for a moment. Her eyes found his. She was flirting; she was terrified.

"I'll see you soon, Mrs. Wegland," Baylor said. Turning back to his car, he called out to his two uniformed colleagues, "*Kom, ons loop.*"

THERE WAS no one to meet them at Heathrow. In a bathroom stall, Dick took almost all the cash from his carry-on and gave it to Henry, who protested, but Dunningham insisted. His family could help him, now that he was here. They hugged, and told each other it would all be okay. They had made it. They were free. Dick would send word to Daisy and Sarah. He knew a professor at the LSE who would telephone a friend in South Africa, who in turn would pass on the message for their wives.

Henry watched his friend walk out of the arrivals lounge. Then he ate bangers and mash and read the *Guardian*. Wolpe and Goldreich had escaped, and Kantor had been arrested. That night he boarded a Pan American Boeing 720 bound for Idlewild Airport.

Exactly ten days after the Liliesleaf arrests, Henry checked into the Hotel Dressler in New York.

28. Confession

"Why wouldn't you tell him? He's your son."

"And you're his wife, Holly. There's no difference."

"I don't believe that."

They were in the kitchen. They'd eaten a quick breakfast together and said good-bye to Glenn. Henry's side throbbed—he pictured a red-hot metal rod wedged between his lower back and tailbone—and he'd had some difficulty getting down the stairs, but when she'd offered to take him to the doctor, he told her she was being silly. Holly cradled her mug in her hands. She looked as if she hadn't slept much.

"I think you know why I'm not going to tell Glenn," Henry said.

"Because you want us to stay together. Because of Saul."

"That too."

"Because you had an affair once, and you wish someone hadn't told Sarah about it, or wish Glenn hadn't found out. Or you don't think you have the moral authority. But you do, you know. It doesn't matter. People in glass houses throw stones all the time."

"I know," Henry said, smiling at the image in his head, a street of shattered glass houses. "But in this case, I don't think it would help anyone. I didn't see anything yesterday. End of story. If Glenn finds out, he finds out. If you want to tell him, that's fine."

"Do you think I should?"

"I think—well, personally, I think you should do what it takes to stay together. If that's what you want, of course. I'm pretty sure that's what he wants."

"This is difficult for you."

"It's not a conversation I'd ever imagined myself having."

"You're doing fine."

"Thank you. You too."

"So, what do you want, Henry?"

"What do I want? I want my arse to stop hurting. I want a thirty-year-old girlfriend and a lot of money. Sorry, bad joke."

"I'll see what I can do." She stuck out her tongue and flashed a silly smile.

After a while she said, "Can I ask why you had an affair? I've always wondered."

"Does anyone know why? Like you said, I suppose. Just happened. And I was in love with her. If that makes a difference, which it does, I think. Remarkable woman. She was brave and clever and very beautiful. I loved Sarah, too, of course."

"What was her name?"

"Nellie Mkhatshwa."

"Hang on. Nellie, as in Nellie and Zeke, the people you sent Saul to see, near Nelspruit. He said he met Lillian . . ."

"One of Nellie's granddaughters."

"But why now? Haven't you seen her since then?"

"I have. But we'd lost touch. Or rather, I hadn't heard from her. And that's what Saul found out—that she died." He pictured Nellie sitting on Colin Beswick's blue fountain, lying on the guest cottage bed. *Izandla ezinhle.* He felt his throat constrict as he imagined a funeral, a circle of mourners under a hot sun.

"So why do you want Saul to meet her family? Aren't you worried he'll find out?"

"I'm fairly certain he'll find out. He's a grown-up now, he can make up his own mind about his philandering gramps. As for my motives—simple, really. I want to know where her children and grandchildren are because I want them to be in my will. They don't have a lot of money, and a small amount could change their lives. And possibly I thought they might be nice people for Glenn to know."

"Oh, Henry."

"Don't 'oh Henry' me."

"Oh, Henry."

29. Fifty-Third and Lex

On hot Lexington Avenue the subway pipes belched steam, moist and grey. In America he was hesitant, uncertain. He kept forgetting what side of the road cars drove on, couldn't understand what people said half the time, had trouble telling nickels from dimes, got a cold drink when he asked for tea. They were crazy for lemonade and ice, wore bright clothing, drove cars with fins, ate hamburgers and milkshakes. New York, New York. People everywhere, skin, sweat gleaming on bare arms and legs, women in short skirts and sunglasses, men in short-sleeved shirts. *How the West Was Won* was playing at the Marquis. Tall black letters across an illuminated white strip. His big hollow heart.

He couldn't shake the feeling that something had gone horribly wrong, that he was in the wrong place, adrift, floating farther and farther away from everything he held dear. He had not talked to Sarah, hadn't spoken to anyone from home. He couldn't phone, couldn't risk endangering anyone. The spy out in the cold. Only, there was no going home. Only, it was stinking hot. A humid heat that made your arse sweat and produced a second skin, a film of moisture that clung to your body. Thank God for air-conditioning, another thing Americans loved.

The euphoria of escape. He was alive, was not going to be arrested or beaten or killed. He had slipped through their hands, outfoxed the South African police. But behind it lurked the loneliness of arrival, the escapee far from home. All the things he couldn't fix, the broken pieces, the broken past that he could neither reconcile nor rebuild—his life and Sarah's, Glenn's, Nellie's. Marooned in America, he was unable to make amends.

He ate in a luncheonette on Broadway, then walked back to the hotel. On Forty-Second Street music spilled out of the bars. High above him the skyscrapers presided, luminous in the afternoon sunlight.

All through the war he'd waited, imagining that one day he'd hear the doorbell and Uncle Isaac would be standing there, smelling of the lavender water he always splashed on his chest after their swims. His mother had promised him, explained that Uncle Isaac had returned to Lithuania, and assured Henry that she'd invited him to stay with them in Port Elizabeth, begged him, implored him. Weeks and months went by, and still Henry waited. Sometimes he thought he saw him crossing the street, or sitting in a tea room, but when the man turned round it wasn't Isaac but a younger man, a stranger with a scrunched-up face and beady eyes.

Back in his room, he turned on the television. The presenters read the news in agitated tones. TV was a new experience for him; he liked their slick American accents, the big maps and graphics behind them. From his hotel aerie he could see across the avenue—people working in their offices, a building under construction, workers in hard hats riding up and down in a caged lift.

After a while, he switched off the TV and listened to some music. Other than some clothes and food, the battery-powered Philips cassette player and three cassettes (Bob Dylan, Miles Davis, Donovan) were the only purchases he'd made. *House Of the Risin' Sun. Alone Together. Belated Forgiveness Plea.*

He'd put his photographs on the dresser, and now stood looking at them, holding each one in turn, studying it, then putting it back. Sarah leaning over Glenn in the garden,

Glenn's little hand on her wrist. The three of them at the Vaal River. There was one other photograph he kept with his papers, small, unframed, and he took it out now as well. Nellie smiling her shy smile, cut out of a larger photo, probably one that included Zeke. It was all so long ago, so far away—the photographs, his past. Here and there. Now and then. History was what happened in between.

AFTERWARDS, AFTER the police had left and she'd gone inside and made tea, holding onto the kitchen counter to steady her shaking hands, Sarah thought that everything would be different, but it wasn't. Except that the adrenaline made the light brighter and the hissing of the electric kettle louder, the world seemed, oddly, just about the same. The tea tasted exactly like tea; the little ridge inside the handle of the teacup was still there, and the sound of Glenn playing in his room upstairs was the same as it always was. It was only when she felt an itch along her nose and a tightness in her eyes that she realised she was crying. A tear plopped into her teacup, and she wiped her eyes with a dishcloth and sat down. It struck her that everything was, in fact, inexorably different, and a loud sob erupted from deep inside her. She sat there, crying and looking at the teacup and the clean bright kitchen and hoping Glenn wouldn't come downstairs. After a while she stood up, patted her cheeks and straightened her skirt, and went upstairs and hugged her child. She kissed his pineapple-scented hair. He let her hold him tight for a minute before he pulled away, frowning slightly. He pointed at the model plane on the cardboard box in front of him.

"Ma, I finished the Spitfire."

"I see that. It's lovely."

"I just have to put the stickers on the wings."

"Glenn, Daddy can't come and visit us yet, so we'll go and visit him. How does that sound?"

"Good. Where?"

"New York, of course. Maybe you'll go first. I have to take care of some things first."

"But, Mom, I don't want to fly all by myself. I'm too young."

"No you're not. You're a big boy now."

EVENING. HE'D been in America three whole days. He walked down Lexington, found his way to a bar, and ordered a whiskey. Drank it quickly and ordered another. The TV jabbered, high above the mirrored shelves of bottles. In Alabama, the police armed with dogs and cattle prods had quashed a civil rights march. It was familiar; it was not familiar. Here, it was on the news, on television, in the newspapers. President Kennedy declared civil rights a "moral issue."

At the end of the bar, a drunk man flirted with two women. When Henry looked at the TV again, someone had changed the channel. A basketball game, blacks and whites playing together on the court. The sight of it made him inexplicably sad.

A while later, a man sat down beside him. Sinewy and tall, with a tanned face and bright white teeth.

"This seat taken?"

"No. Go ahead."

The man ordered a beer, which arrived ice cold in a frosted mug.

"Galen." He thrust out his hand.

"Henry. How do you do."

"You're not from around here."

"No. I'm from South Africa."

"Heard of it. Couldn't find it on a map, though." The man smiled, flashing his long teeth. "I'm not from around here either. Oklahoma."

"Galen. That's a funny name for an American."

"Well, I'm a funny American. Just kidding, pal. My mother's Greek, my dad's Scottish."

They clinked glasses, and the man looked up at the TV and surveyed the bar. He asked Henry how he liked New York, and Henry replied, somewhat automatically, that it was a wonderful city. He wanted to tell him his wife and son weren't with him and he hadn't spoken to friend or family in over a week. But he couldn't say it, couldn't explain. He couldn't even say their names, or Nellie's. He wanted to say them all out loud, to feel their names on his lips and speak his sprawling fears. But that was impossible. He was a fugitive, a secret person. So he said nothing, just smiled and sipped his drink. He'd become accustomed to not revealing the truth. Some part of him was still in flight. He had arrived nowhere. He thought about the word immigrant. It had a lost, flotsamy sound.

Meanwhile, New York. Big, bustling, vertical, hot. It rushed at you, Checker cabs thudded over manholes, loud men walking fast, everyone in a rush. He liked the yawny, foghorn accents, the hats men wore, the hurrying legs of women on Fifth Avenue, the billboards and neon signs, the music, the looming skyscrapers that Glenn would have marvelled at. Henry slept, shaved, ate, watched television. He collected shiny quarters but made no phone calls, just stashed them in a drawer with his socks and underpants. They had agreed: don't talk unless it was an emergency.

A yellow clown sold hamburgers on television. Teams called Tigers and Lions played American football in helmets and pads. He watched it all in his little hotel room, and pictured stuffed animals, fluffy bears with rub-me noses, and thought of Glenn, and he gulped quick draughts of air. A phantom scent of his son's skin filled his nostrils, and he reeled, stranded on his hotel bed, too lost to weep. *Lala ngenxeba*, the Africans said. Lie on the wound.

HE RODE a commuter train to White Plains to visit Bob and Gail Gornick, the only South Africans he knew anywhere near New York. Bob was a lawyer, had told Henry long ago that America was the place to be. The economy was booming. Henry hadn't moved halfway across the world to end up back in Liverpool—or even London—but now he wasn't so sure. Dick was in London, and so were a lot of other people he knew. Bob poured him a drink and apologised that they wouldn't be having a braai. In the garden, the Gornick boys were tossing around an American football—like a narrow rugby ball. Inside the house, the books and furniture, even the cups and saucers, reminded him of his own house, and all the houses he'd left behind.

"When will Sarah and Glenn join you?" Gail asked.

"Soon, I hope."

They ate roast beef and potatoes, and then the boys went upstairs. Henry could tell his hosts wanted to hear his story, but he didn't know what to tell them. "So much has happened, so fast," he said, reminding them not to tell anyone of his whereabouts. No, of course not, they promised. And he could tell they were picturing it, their past lives, their families, but it was far away. For them.

They told him he could stay with them. But there wasn't enough space in their ranch-style house—cluttered, two children, a cat.

Bob said, "We'll put in a swimming pool next summer. You'll bring Sarah and Glenn. He'll play with our boys."

"They don't say 'costume' here, they say 'swimsuit,'" Gail said.

A lull, and then Bob said: "Waiter, what's this fly doing in my soup? Looks like the breaststroke to me, sir."

Henry forced a laugh. But he felt lost, unravelled. He had the sense that it would all begin again, that at any moment, this house—the chair he was sitting on, the trees outside—would disappear, and he'd be running again, waiting, travelling incognito: the exile in flight.

The day long ago, after he'd rescued her, Sarah's father and brother had dropped her off at the tea room in the King George Hotel. The waiter brought tea and scones, and Henry found himself talking easily, gazing into her green eyes, following the graceful movements of her hands. They lived in Johannesburg; her father was a silversmith, had his own shop on Jeppe Street. Sarah played the piano, her mother the violin, her sister Esther the flute and violin, and Meyer and Isadore were tenors in the *shul* choir. Of course she was a pianist, he'd thought, admiring her long fingers. Alert eyes, auburn hair, shiny as a farthing. Something about her made him feel at ease, made him want to smile. Her silk blouse reminded him of a flower, a lily perhaps. Elegant features, high cheekbones, a Barbara Stanwyck smile. She loved jazz. "Do you know Oscar Peterson?" she asked, and when Henry said he did her eyes lit up. He liked the passion that music, chocolate cake, a joke, stirred in her, liked the way she stared at him as they talked, not sombre but serious, the warmth in her eyes, and her easy smile.

Back in Johannesburg, they went dancing, talked a lot, laughed a lot. And when, one evening, he mustered the courage to kiss her while they were walking back to the car, she put a cool hand on his arm and kissed him back.

When he'd left Meyer and Aniela's house after those long nights in their garage, Meyer had looked at him with unapologetic wrath, for putting their daughter in harm's way, for doing whatever it was that forced him to flee like a common criminal. That's how his own parents would view it, too; his anxious, protective mother would curse his arrogance and stupidity. How she must have hated not knowing where he was at the time—locked up in a jail, perhaps, like Rusty and the others. But now she knew he was safe, at least.

HE WALKED out of a matinee, *The Thrill of it All,* surrounded by teenagers blinking in the bright sun on Broadway. Strangers, heat. Back at the hotel, the lobby was crowded. Bellhops rushed in and out as tourists waited to check in. The antimacassared armchairs were full of young men in grey suits engaged in urgent conversation, checking their watches or distractedly reading the afternoon papers. Everyone looked elegant, prosperous, rushed. Only Henry had nowhere to go.

He wandered the insouciant streets. New York didn't seem to need the rest of the world, or even care much about its existence. And no one in the world knew where he was right now. As dusk fell, he walked slowly back to the hotel, a lone animal in the gathering gloom.

He lay on his bed that night, remembering his mother's letters sent to friends and family in Lithuania and Liverpool, pleading for Isaac to join them or go to Palestine; all unanswered. The war was long over when a telegram arrived one day, followed by a man they'd known in Shadowa. He told them that Isaac had joined the resistance, that he and his comrades had stolen munitions and made bombs and blown up trains and bridges—until one day the Germans had arrived in trucks and armoured cars. They'd shot at beds and closets, fired at cupboards and floorboards, walls and ceilings, and then came the flame-throwers and then came the flames, and finally they'd hurled grenades until the buildings lay smouldering and ruined. There was no way Isaac could have survived, their visitor said.

Like Isaac, Henry and his comrades had seen only one version of the future, the better world, hadn't permitted thoughts of failure, of lives sacrificed, lost, destroyed. Of course, he was one of the lucky ones. He wasn't dead or in jail awaiting trial or hiding in a cellar. He was here, on the fourteenth floor of a hotel, looking down on a river of cars and people—free, but a long way from home, banished from his former life, a sort of human black hole, gravity pulling him into himself, even as he stood staring at the flux of the street below.

His eleventh day in America, Henry broke the rule. He took the shiny quarters to a pay phone and dialled a Johannesburg number.

"Hello."

"Sarah. My Sarah. I love you," he said quickly. "I long to see you. Hurry."

"Me too," she said softly. And then, "Are you okay? Is anything the matter?"

"Fine. I just wanted to hear your voice."

"Good. But we can't talk like this. It's not safe. Don't worry about me, okay? I love you." And then she put down the phone.

She was right to hang up. You never knew who might be listening. They couldn't take any chances.

Crying, he walked back to the Hotel Dressler.

30. FREEDOM

Bonga drove him back to number 932 Modisana Road. Saul clasped Vusi's hand when he met them at the car. He didn't know what to say.

"You did it," he managed at last. "Thank you." Even as he said it, the words sounded inadequate.

Vusi smiled. "You did it too, bra."

Bonga spoke to Vusi, and Saul went inside. He gave Lillian a hug on his way to the bathroom, where he took a piss, splashed some water on his face, and studied himself in the mirror. He was alive. He'd never been so happy to see his pimples and blemishes, his own grateful eyes staring back at him.

When he returned outside, he found Bonga sitting on the lawn with Vusi and Ndolo. Bonga leaned back on his hands as he watched Dimpho play with her Pick n Pay dolls, and Saul sat down beside him.

"Really, thank you," he said. "Both of you. That was incredible."

Vusi shook his head. "Don't thank us. I'm sorry for what happened. And don't worry about Sipho and the *tsotsis*. We'll take care of them. We'll move you to another hotel. We don't want them coming after you."

Lillian joined them, and they all sat under the tree in a loose semicircle around Dimpho, taking turns with the princess dolls, making them talk and dance and jump. Dimpho shrieked with joy. She'd forgotten all about the guns.

After Bonga left, they discussed logistics. Vusi suggested they collect Saul's suitcase and find another hotel on the way to Kruger Park. Saul said it would be his treat; they could all stay there for the night. Then he remembered Dunningham's invitation to stay at his game farm; he didn't know where it was exactly, somewhere near the Park, which he guessed covered an area the size of Rhode Island, but still, it was worth a try. He phoned Dunningham, standing in a corner of the garden as he spoke to him. Yes, he was welcome to use the house; it wasn't far from Nelspruit, just an hour or so. And bring some friends? Yes, of course. There was a house-keeper and maybe one other person who might be staying there. Saul said he didn't want to impose, but Dunningham insisted.

"You'll be doing me a favour," the man who sounded a lot like Gramps said. "We don't use that place enough. I'll call the housekeeper and tell him to make sure the house is open and buy some groceries. Everything okay?"

"Yeah, great," Saul said. "Never better."

31. NIGHT AT GERDE'S

"I'm calling with some news." The man had an American accent, said his name was Jim Novo. The last link in a convoluted chain, a friend of a friend of a friend, with no knowledge of the import of the news he was relaying.

"It's not good. Sarah's been arrested. The boy is safe, with friends. That's all I know." Then he hung up.

Not good? It was bloody terrible. Sarah? Arrested? The Ninety Day Detention Act meant they could arrest anyone. Had he caused this? By phoning her? By running away in the first place? What would he do if they told him to come back and stand trial or they'd throw the book at his wife? And what about Glenn? Safe, where? Who was he with? For now, it seemed there was nothing Henry could do. He couldn't even find out any more information. He could only wait there in the loud silence of his hotel room, a million miles away.

He would get a message to Sarah's brother. Get her out. Whatever it cost. Her parents would pitch in, his parents, brother, the Dunninghams could all be counted on. She'd write to the Chief Magistrate and request permission after she'd served her ninety days. A trip to Rhodesia, perhaps. But he knew that this was a long shot, given that her husband had fled. Maybe a boat or private plane to Windhoek? They might hold her in the hope of forcing him to return. And he would. If they wanted to make a swap, he would do it: his freedom for hers and Glenn's.

He drifted in and out of sleep that night, and she murmured to him in his dreams, but he couldn't make out the words, nor could he shake the hazy image from his waking mind—Sarah, behind bars, in a cold prison cell. He got up and watched the red stream of taillights down the avenue. White women were probably treated better than other prisoners, but they were still prisoners, still in prison. Sarah would be cold. She was always cold. She wouldn't be able to sleep on a hard mattress with a thin prison blanket. He couldn't forgive himself for not being there to stop it from happening or, at the very least, to fight on her behalf, to visit and bring her food and clothes—and he knew he'd never be able to.

THE SUBWAY—loud, metallic—rattled through dark tunnels and took him from the suits and doormen of Lexington Avenue to the jeans and long hair of Greenwich Village. There, he walked, occasionally pausing at the shop windows on Eighth Street—a bookshop, deli, a newsagent, a dark storefront with opaque windows and no sign.

Joe Borgese had arranged to meet Henry at Kettle of Fish on MacDougal Street. The narrow bar was crowded and smoke-filled. Joe was amiable, with tufty black hair, long limbs, and a round, boyish face. Constantly in motion, his hands floated and gesticulated as he spoke. The beer was cold, and there was good music on the jukebox. Joe explained that he taught anthropology at a university called the New School. It all sounded rather made-up to Henry, and Joe's floral shirt and denim jacket confirmed that he was a peculiarly American species of academic.

"It's really great to meet you, man." This was as close as Henry had come to a welcome to the country he found mostly baffling.

They ate dinner at the Deli-Box on Bleecker Street. Steamy windows, the smell of hamburgers and bacon fat. Borgese spoke about music, activism, sociology. He called himself a Trotskyite, loved poetry and folk music.

"Things are happening in your country," he said. "You can feel it. Am I right? Change is in the air everywhere. It's a good thing."

"Yes. A good thing," Henry agreed. And a dangerous thing, too.

"To the Struggle."

Henry nodded, and they clinked beers. He felt burdened, had for some time now, by some dark animal clinging to his back. It wasn't the feeling of being watched anymore, a quarry. He could stop looking for tails when he took a cab on Broadway. No, it was something vaguer, heavier: his complicity or guilt, the weight of distance and displacement. He ate his cheeseburger.

Borgese said he'd been expecting an academic. "That's cool, though. Not too many cats I know are lawyers." Cats. Henry smiled. It was hard not to like the guy. He spoke about the Kaluli people of Papua New Guinea, whom he had visited while researching his PhD. Were anthropologists in South Africa occupied with these issues? Or was it an American luxury to fight for civil rights and also worry about how Pacific islanders caught fish and built their huts? Henry was beginning to suspect something about America, beginning to comprehend its vastness, the intricacies of its scope. It was an empire unto itself.

They strolled through Washington Square as the sun set above rooftops and water towers. Borgese turned to Henry while they were walking.

"I just want to say. Whatever it was you did, you guys are heroes man."

"I'm no hero. My wife is in prison."

Borgese led the way to Gerde's Folk City on West Fourth Street. The narrow door opened onto a small vestibule, then another door squeaked open and they were in a large dim room, full of happy faces. A group was already waiting at a small table near the stage with a pitcher of beer. A tall woman with black hair and black eye makeup introduced herself to Henry as a field agent for the Congress of Racial Equality, reporting on violence against civil rights workers down south. She gestured to her boyfriend, a foreign student from Guatemala, and a young black man, a poet. A whole new America, Henry suspected, this Greenwich Village underground. The CORE woman talked about gathering evidence, publishing offenders' names. In America the press was free. No secret meetings here. The law was—at least nominally—on their side. Very dramatic, America, Henry thought to himself. A hyperbolic country, lived in neon poetry. Everything was instant, deluxe, super, fast, do-it-yourself, loud. Five channels on TV. He'd never seen a car as big as a Cadillac or a store as vast as Macy's.

A man and a woman took the stage, he with a guitar, she with wood maracas; her voice trembled above his cowboy twang. Henry drank his beer and smiled at Borgese. They listened to a few songs, and then Joe led Henry outside, taking a joint from his wallet and lighting up in a darkened doorway. Took a hit, then handed it to Henry. The dagga made his throat itch, but soon his head felt cottony and soft and the strawberry sky above the rooftops went radiant and glittery. Even the tenements looked beautiful, their dark-red brick, fire-escape ladders like stacked black zeds, warm yellow light oozing from the windows. Also the stranded feeling again. What was Sarah doing right now, in her cold dark cell? What did they tell Glenn when he asked where his dad had gone?

"You all right?" Borgese took another pull. Smoke snaked into the sky.

"Yes. A long way from home, that's all."

Back inside, a skinny kid with wide eyes and a scraggly blond beard took the stage, looking down at his guitar as he sang. "I'm going where the water tastes like wine. And I ain't gonna be treated this way."

THE PHONE startled him.

"Hello, is this Mr. Jones?" *Misterrrr*. Fake American accent, he could tell right off. Special Branch? Informer? Friend?

Before Henry could say no, the voice at the other end said, "My name is Gerrit Deurmekaar, from Alaska Booksellers." *Fraahm*. *Deurmekaar,* as in confused. Then Henry knew, and smiled.

"Hi, Gerrit, how are you?" Henry felt that he might cry, so happy was he to hear his old friend's voice.

"I'm doing fine. Listen, we have a book to deliver to you. The package should arrive on Tuesday."

"Arrive where?"

"Same place as the first book we shipped out. *The Vels-koen Litvak*, I believe it was. Okay, bye now."

32. HOME

Henry ate lunch at the diner, hobbled home, took a nap. Despite the throbbing pain in his right leg, he went for a walk that evening along Prospect Park West, past the red sand-stone and terracotta townhouses, past the Victorian brown-stones and apartment towers, and into the park. It had rained the night before, and water lay in pools on the macadam and on the lawn. A woman in red boots pushed a stroller and talked on her cell phone.

When he got back to the house, Holly wasn't there. Glenn was sitting at the table reading the newspaper. He hadn't turned on the lights, and the downstairs rooms were washed with the marmalade glow of the living-room lamps. There was something slightly unusual about it all, something askew— Glenn home alone, no sign of Holly or supper, only the lamps switched on.

"Holly upstairs?" Henry asked. He hadn't seen her since he'd left for lunch.

"Um, no, gone," Glenn said. And then: "She's staying with a friend for the night, actually."

"Oh?"

"Yeah. Oh." Glenn folded the newspaper, pushed it away from him. "Why didn't you tell me, Dad?"

Kak and shit, he thought. "Tell you what?"

"Everything. Why do you think you need to keep things from me? Are you trying to protect her? Or me? Or yourself?"

"I don't know," Henry said. He sat down at the table. His son glowered at him, then looked away. "I'm sorry."

"Everyone with their fucking secrets. She didn't want to tell me, said she promised you she wouldn't. But she was lying in bed crying."

They sat there, not talking for a while. Henry tried to think of things to say, massaged his leg.

"I am," he said, "really sorry."

Glenn nodded, looked at his newspaper, jaw clenched. After a while he said, "We may as well eat."

He ordered Thai food. While they waited for the delivery, Henry went upstairs to hang up his coat and put on slippers. The painkillers were helping, but it still hurt to take the stairs. When he came back down, Glenn had set the table for two.

The food arrived, and Glenn served and poured them each a glass of wine.

"Okay," he said, his mouth full of lemongrass chicken. "Let's talk." He chewed slowly, put his knife and fork down, squeezed his hands together.

"Good," Henry said.

"I want to sell the house." Glenn spoke to his plate. "I've talked to Holly about it."

"I see. Wow. May I ask why?"

"Because we need a change. Saul is gone. Holly is obviously bored. It'll be her choice if she wants to come or not. I'm not going to make her. But I'm putting the house on the market either way."

His voice like shards of glass. Maybe he'd known all along, or maybe she'd told him just today. Anyway, it was all out in the open now.

There was a part of Glenn that hated Holly, Henry thought, as he spooned some chicken from the tinfoil tub. Sarah was partially to blame, as was Henry of course. Abandonment, secrecy, infidelity, being kept in the dark—everything Glenn feared and despised had converged on him. Two slices of green pepper were stuck to a piece of chicken, and Henry picked them off with his fingers but couldn't find a spare plate to put them on. He hesitated, then plopped them back in the foil tub.

"I'm not sure if I think it's a good idea," he said. "Moving, right now. Just like that."

"I'm not sure if I give a shit what you think. This is not your decision, okay."

There was a part of Glenn that hated Henry too, wasn't there? For the wrongs he'd committed that Glenn hadn't known were wrong at the time, for getting them into the mess that caused first Henry and then Sarah to abandon him, forcing him to cling to his father, a flotsam kid and his flotsam dad, adrift in America. Glenn hadn't allowed himself to hate Henry, not then, not when Henry was all he had. And it was Henry's greatest fear that Glenn would fail or be unhappy and it would all be his fault.

Glenn squeezed the handle of his fork in his palm. "Don't tell me what to do. You don't make decisions for me. And you don't keep secrets from me. Am I clear?"

"Yes, of course."

He wondered if Glenn might throw something, really yell, smash a plate. It was okay. It was salutary. Let it come down.

But Glenn was quiet now, breathing heavily through his nostrils, as if he'd just come in from a jog. Nothing would be thrown, nothing broken. Glenn couldn't ride his anger for long enough to do anything like that. A sense of loss washed over Henry. He'd mucked things up, hadn't been a very good dad. That Glenn had turned out so well and was such a good father himself had as much to do with fortitude on Glenn's part as Henry's parenting. He'd tried, of course, but a single father in a strange country is bound to blunder. And despite what Sarah had said, you can't be a mother from the other side of the world.

"You're right," Henry said. "Your house, your choice. I'm sure you're doing the right thing."

"Don't be so sure. But it's what I want to do." Glenn took a sip of wine, then another. He frowned at the food on his plate as if it too had wronged him. "How's your back?"

"It's okay. It'll be okay."

Glenn had that lonely look on his face, full of silence.

"I've known for some time," he said after a while. "I didn't know for sure. But I suspected. Some things, when you think they might be true, it's because they are true. She said you saw Jonathan here, and she didn't want to put you in a difficult position, you know, not telling me."

Henry nodded. That was very decent of Holly. But why? She knew that she could trust him. Maybe it was for the better. Everything out in the open.

"Can I ask you something?" Henry said.

"Ask."

"You're not doing this to be vindictive?"

"Doing what?"

"Selling the house, packing up, moving."

"No. For fuck's sake. It's not about you, and it's not about Holly. I've been putting it off too long. Well, not anymore."

"Glenn, I only want you to be happy."

"We can only do what we can do, under the circumstances."

He saw now that Glenn had the will to persist, the will to endure. Perhaps it was in their blood.

Glenn was leaning back in his chair now. The anger had drained from his face.

"Where will you go?" Henry asked.

"Upstate. Remember we went to the Holdens' house up near Bard College. Well, somewhere like that. I can run a small practice from home. Nice place for Saul to visit during the holidays. My only concern is you, Dad."

"Please don't concern yourself about me."

Glenn was entitled to this, to try again for happiness. Henry didn't want to stop him. Couldn't stop him. But it would be a change, that's for sure. He'd find a place for himself in Manhattan, a one-bedroom in the Village maybe, or live in the

Red Hook apartment. Though Glenn probably wanted him to move to one of those old folks communities in Westchester. Sit around and play bingo with dusty old geezers waiting to die. Never. Not going to happen. He didn't mind the idea of living in Red Hook. A bit isolated, but the apartments were big enough, faced south, light-filled, he'd heard Glenn say a hundred times. Or were they west-facing? He remembered the day they'd seen the building for the first time. Glenn had rented a car and the three of them had driven to look at Gowanus and Red Hook. I love the emptiness, Glenn had said. You're on the edge of the city. He could walk to the river; he could walk to Brooklyn Heights. He'd be okay. Of course it wasn't where he'd imagined getting old. He hadn't imagined a lot of things, but they happened anyway. Life turned out that way: surprising.

33. Package at JFK

There were three flights from London to New York every day. The earliest arrived at two P.M., and the last one at seven. Henry showered and shaved, ate breakfast in the hotel restaurant, then took a taxi to the airport.

The Pan Am Worldport was a flying saucer of glass, metal, and concrete, lashed to the earth by steel cables and cement girders. Glenn's type of building, he thought. Glenn, who loved the Brixton radio tower, who drew intricate sketches of skyscrapers in the margins of his schoolbooks. In the arrivals lounge, Henry drank a soda from a paper cup filled to the brim with ice, watched businessmen come and go, families reuniting.

He waited across the walkway when the first flight landed. Just in case it was a trap, in case the phone was bugged and someone had guessed Dunningham's meaning. Didn't want to be a sitting duck. He watched the passengers disembark. The last passenger, an old woman with grey hair and a walker, was met by a young man in a blue-and-white jacket.

He walked around the airport, ate a Hershey's Bar, read the newspaper. At four o'clock he was at another gate, waiting. The place was full of light, bright fluorescent light that cascaded into the vastness, and it was into this electric glare that he saw Dunningham emerge from the plane, slightly stooped, listing a bit to his right side. And then he saw the boy beside him, holding Dick's right hand, looking very solemn, a Pan

Am bag slung over his right shoulder. His jaw was clenched and his hair was longer than usual.

Henry rushed over to them. He picked Glenn up and hugged him tight. He was bigger, heavier, but he smelled the same, his little-boy smell of linseed and soap.

"Dad, I flew eight thousand miles. I spoke to the captain."

"God, it's good to see you. Both of you."

Dunningham clapped Henry on the back and gave him a bear hug. Glenn insisted on carrying his own bag as they walked together to baggage claim.

"He's been a wonderful travel companion," Dunningham said. "Good as gold."

THEY PILED into a taxi and sped from Idlewild through the brown brick sprawl. Glenn looked out eagerly.

"When's Mommy coming?" They were crossing the Queensboro Bridge.

"Soon."

"Tomorrow?"

"Not tomorrow, maybe a few days. We'll phone her."

The ebullience drained from Glenn's face and he looked weary and worried, a little old man suddenly, sitting hunched, his narrow shoulder tucked under Henry's arm.

At the hotel, Glenn fell asleep on Henry's bed, still fully clothed. Henry drew the blanket around him, and he and Dick watched the boy sleep as they talked quietly. A cousin of Helen Joseph's had flown with Glenn to London. About Sarah, Dick knew only that the police had found banned material in the house. A mutual friend, Archie Lewitton, had visited her in prison, and said she was fine, a bit thin but fine. Yes, it was true that Wolpe and Goldreich had escaped. No news of the others, though, and no date had been set for the trial—the state had yet to file the formal indictment. Daisy had slipped out through Rhodesia and joined Dick in London.

"Daisy gave me this letter." Dick drew an envelope from his pocket. "From Sarah."

The letter was addressed to Daisy and written so that it would pass the prison's censors, but was clearly intended for other eyes—Henry's eyes.

My dear Daisy,

Know that I am all right. I am being treated decently and have enough to eat. I will keep my sanity and my health. Don't be cross, and please don't worry.

My cell is approximately ten by eight feet. There is a table and a wooden chair and a sanitary pot. Not much in the way of luxury, but it is enough. I sleep on blankets and a felt mat that I roll up every morning at six. There is a small window and a light behind wire mesh recessed into the wall. The nights are long. There is nothing to read except the Bible. We are allowed to exercise in the yard twice a day, for half an hour each time, sometimes a bit longer, and during that time we are allowed to talk quietly, as long as everyone behaves. I have tried meditation, and so far I've failed at it. It's conversation that I long for. To be part of people again.

Some bad news. I was six weeks pregnant when I got here, and I miscarried. I was taken to the prison hospital so I had a doctor present. I'm fine now, a bit weak and a bit tired and a bit sad, that's all.

Thank you for the warm clothing. I can't wait to talk to you again. In the meantime, can I ask you to visit Glenn for me? Tell him that I love him and miss him and that I will see him soon.

Much love,
Sarah

Henry read the letter through twice, then sat staring at Sarah's small swirly handwriting on the thin paper. How big is a foetus at six weeks? A little butter bean huddled in her womb. He pictured bootees and bibs, a pram with chrome wheels. A child, a brother or sister for Glenn. Gone. Is that why she didn't mention Henry by name? Was she worried that if she wrote his name the letter wouldn't pass the prison censors? Or was it a rebuke? So much had gone wrong. And it was all his fault.

"Have you read it?" Henry asked.

"Yes. She didn't know she was pregnant. You had no way of knowing."

Henry said nothing, stared at the letter.

"She's tough, Hen. Her mom's been visiting, so have friends, family. They brought her clothes, even some food. She probably won't serve out her ninety days."

"All because of a few books? Some bloody magazines or papers? It's preposterous."

"Archie thinks—"

"We were so careful."

Dunningham's mouth puckered, as if he'd bitten something sour.

"What, Dick? What does Archie think?"

"Archie reckons she bought Glenn's freedom with her own."

"What do you mean?"

"They let Glenn leave. He flew under his own passport to London. Maybe Sarah made a deal with the police and couldn't keep her end of the bargain. Maybe she never intended to. Promised them something she knew she couldn't, or wouldn't, give them. That's what Archie thinks. Apparently she sent Janey and Ndimande home, so she must have known they'd detain her. Had a bag already packed when they searched the house, found the banned stuff, and booked her."

"Oh, Jesus. What have I done?"

"Hen, what could you do? They can't keep her in prison, or in the country, you know that. They've got nothing on her. She was adamant you shouldn't return and she was desperate for Glenn to get out."

He didn't tell Dick that he'd phoned her. But the conversation, her end of it, took on a different meaning now. *Don't worry about me.* She knew she'd be arrested.

Soft auburn ringlets. Tiny fingers. They'd long ago decided on Ella or Grace if they had a girl. When he'd thought about having another child, he'd always imagined a girl. He pictured a silver baby rattle, holding her up in his arms and kissing her with the blue sky as his witness.

THE NEXT day they walked to Times Square. Glenn was giddy, timid, and excited at the same time—enraptured by the skyscrapers with their spires and pinnacles, the colours, the whirl of pedestrians. Henry thought that his son looked at him differently, with just the slightest reserve, the way a boy might look at a friendly grown-up. But that would change, he told himself. It was all so new and surprising. They ate lunch at a diner on Lexington Avenue. Glenn tucked into his cheeseburger and onion rings and milkshake, and counted the taxi cabs idling at the traffic light.

"Wow, this is a busy city," he said as they walked back to the hotel.

"Busy and hot and wonderful. Can you believe this heat? So humid."

"I know. It feels like it's going to rain. Dad," his voice had gone quiet. "How many days? Till Mommy comes?"

"Soon, boy, soon. I don't know how many days exactly. Tomorrow we're going to the top of the world's tallest building. How does that sound?"

"Okay," was all he said.

But Henry knew that she wouldn't be there soon. What banned magazine had they found in the house? They'd been so careful. Not that it really mattered. The South African police barely needed a reason to detain someone. What mattered was that Sarah was in prison and she'd stay there for ninety days. She'd given herself up, allowed herself to get arrested. For Glenn, for him. She had lost a child in a prison hospital, without her husband beside her, with nobody to hold her hand. That night he watched his son sleep—his eyes burning with unshed tears, his mind full of images of Sarah and prison nurses and baby clothes—until he was too tired to maintain his vigil, and fell asleep himself.

Glenn was in the bathroom, but not in the bath as instructed. Henry knocked, and hearing no reply, opened the heavy door. The boy was hunkered on the edge of the toilet seat, rocking ever so slightly, arms hanging like fins at his side, and when Henry entered he didn't stop or even look up.

"Glenn?"

Still Glenn showed no sign that he'd noticed him.

Henry had never seen his son like this, not even when he was sick. Limbs slack, eyes fixed blankly on the tiled floor.

"Glenn."

"What?"

"Bath. Come on, big boy, it's past your bedtime."

"Okay."

He uncurled his body, slowly, reluctantly, until he was standing, then Henry twisted the tap slowly, and together they watched the restless water fill the tub.

34. Emthunzini

After an hour on the highway and another on a narrow rural road, they were deep in the bush, driving roughly parallel to Kruger National Park, in the middle of Africa, or so it seemed to Saul. They'd passed impala grazing, watched an antelope stroll across the road, big eyes darting, hairy nose twitching. When the car approached, it leaped over the bushes and zigzagged through the *veld*. A rusty Land Rover passed by, its engine clanking loudly. Dimpho suddenly had a lot to say, and Saul guessed she wanted to pee or eat or both. The sudden flutter of tiny birds above the treetops delighted her. The windows were open, and Saul, calmer now and glad to be in the company of others, enjoyed the feeling of the wind in his hair. He held out his arm, moving his hand up and down in waves, as the wind rolled over his fingers.

Then they were on a private road, bumping along past *mopane* and thorn trees and olive-green bushes. The house sat on a hilltop; it was square and modern, painted white, with wooden beams and a wide wraparound verandah.

By nightfall they were seated around the dining table, drinking tea and eating toast and jam. Thick darkness and trilling bush hum outside the house, warm yolky light inside. The oak table was stained with whitish rings from wet glasses. The house itself was *bushveld* modern: cement walls, wide windows, a large living room with brown leather couches and armchairs, and blue cushions scattered on a wooden banquette at a window. Amateur landscapes and framed botanical prints hung on the walls. Apart from the caretaker's house behind the kitchen, a smaller version of the main house, there were no other houses in sight, no lights, only the moon and stars.

Dimpho was stretched out on some cushions, playing with a Barbie doll they'd found in one of the bedrooms. A fellow guest, Londiwe, sat with them, listening to their story. Ndolo did most of the talking, mostly in Zulu. She didn't have to translate. Saul understood—gun, Nedbank, Sipho. While they were talking, Lillian squatted beside Dimpho, singing softly to her until she closed her eyes and her limp hand released the doll. Londiwe told them that her father had once worked on the farm, and she'd grown up nearby. She was studying computers at a technicon near Naperville and came back once in a while to visit friends; whenever she did, she stayed in the house, which the Dunninghams rarely used, she said. With her high cheekbones and forehead, she reminded Saul of Modigliani women he'd seen in art history slides. Prettier though, with kind eyes, and glossy lips she ran her tongue over every now and again. They drank tea and talked, until the gaps in conversation became longer, and the chirruping sounds of the bush were the only sounds in the room.

They cleaned up and washed the dishes, then Lillian scooped up Dimpho, and they reconnoitred the upstairs bedrooms together, assigning Lillian and Dimpho the first room at the top of the stairs while Saul was given a quiet room at the back of the house. The room was small and clean, with only the single bed, an armless chair, and a wooden table for furniture, and a musty smell that reminded him of summer camp. A white alarm clock on the windowsill had long since stopped. When he sat on the bed, he realised he was exhausted.

He fell asleep quickly but woke up with a jerk, having dreamed of a vast airport overrun by a herd of kudu and men with guns riding around on baggage carts. Outside the window, the sky was pierced with bright stars, and he heard distant animal howls and pictured hyenas stalking the hills, staking claim to the night.

HE AWOKE to birdsong and the sound of voices and cooking. They drank coffee and ate scrambled eggs and toast on the broad verandah. The land was vivid in the buzzing sunlight; birds darted about in the trees. Vusi made a few phone calls, but wouldn't say what might happen to their assailants.

"I told you, man, don't worry about those guys. Hey, they won't pull anything like that again."

Londiwe told them that the house was called Emthunzini, which meant "place in the shade." But what she was really interested in was New York, and how to get a job at Apple or Facebook.

In the afternoon, Saul and Londiwe went for a walk. She showed him the electric fence that kept monkeys out, and pointed out porcupine and zebra tracks, and also aloe plants that could save you from dehydration. Farther on, they saw a small herd of impala and a lone wildebeest in a marshy gully, brown and brooding in the *vlei*. As she walked ahead of him, it occurred to Saul that he might get lucky, have sex with Londiwe, and he imagined her full thighs and pictured her naked breasts. A fitting ending after everything that had happened.

She told him about a man who had been fed to a lion. Not far from there. The farmworker had been bound and tied up and dropped over the fence into a lion enclosure at the Mokwalo White Lion Project. A white farmer and three black men had watched as the lion mauled the man and dragged him into the bush. A construction worker saw the men with blood on their shirts and phoned the police, but all they found was the man's skull and shreds of clothing.

They walked back along a dry riverbed, the wrinkled mudbanks sprouting grass and weeds. The breeze carried a sweet silty dust that caught in his nostrils. The bush was teeming, immense and full of secrets.

EVERYONE WAS in the kitchen when they arrived back, helping to cook a lamb stew. Saul offered to make rice and salad, and opened a couple of bottles of wine he found in the pantry— Dunningham didn't seem like the kind of guy who would mind too much.

Vusi and Londiwe didn't like Dunningham's CD collection. A row of Deutsche Grammophon recordings, jazz, Dylan, Joni Mitchell. They put on James Brown: "Stay on the scene . . . like a sex machine."

"But why are you here?" Londiwe said to Saul over supper. "Are you doing work, or just got lost trying to find Plett?"

Everyone laughed.

"No, just taking a look around. My grandfather's from here, my dad was born here. I mean, South Africa, not *here* here."

They all looked at him, waiting for him to continue. Horns and bass throbbed in the speakers.

"I thought maybe I'd try to make a documentary," he said. "But now I don't think so."

"I don't blame you," Vusi said, not unkindly.

"No, not because of what happened. I just don't know what I'd be making it about." He suddenly felt self-conscious.

"The Dunninghams are friends of your grandfather?" Londiwe asked.

"That's right."

"Was he in the Struggle, like Mr. Dunningham?"

"He was, yes."

"Viva Saul's *umkhulu*," she said with a smile.

Vusi swirled the wine around in his glass and made a big show of tasting it. It was all surprisingly comfortable, Saul thought, none of them at home, but everyone at ease, enjoying themselves. He felt expansive and alive and slightly drunk.

"So, your grandfather," Londiwe said. "He sent you to see these guys? He said go to Ka Nyamazane?"

"Pretty much."

"But why?"

"He knew their grandmother."

Lillian and Ndolo giggled. Vusi, who had been looking out the window, turned his attention to them. His eyes widened, and then he raised a hand to his mouth in mock horror. The girls erupted in laughter, and Vusi said something in Zulu.

"Maybe," Ndolo replied.

"I'm asking them," Vusi said, "how come they knew something like that and they never told me."

"You never wondered?" Lillian said mockingly. "Jissus, men are idiots."

"True, true," Vusi said.

"Did you know, Saul?" Ndolo asked.

"Um, no. I was beginning to suspect, though."

The truth was, he hadn't suspected anything, but didn't want to appear to be the last to know. And the reason he hadn't suspected anything was that sex, to Saul, was like God or kabbalah or the Internet—too vast and complex to comprehend fully. It was his own conspiracy theory of sorts: he believed everyone was having sex with everyone else— everyone apart from him, that is—but how, when or why it happened was a complete and utter mystery.

"I know he saw her once," Ndolo said. "When he visited, a long time ago. She stayed with me in Johannesburg. They had lunch together in Rosebank."

Saul tried to picture Henry and Nellie at a restaurant in a shopping mall. Would anyone have guessed they'd been lovers and revolutionaries? They probably thought she was his nurse or something, two old fogeys out for a quiet lunch. What would they have spoken about? After all those years? Knowing Gramps, he probably complained about the food.

"I think they were in love," Ndolo said. "Even though they were both married. Nellie told me about him, and also about her arrest."

"Tell me, please," Saul said.

THE POLICE found Nellie in Jabulani. She was arrested and held for two days before anyone questioned her. A young officer, Baylor, came and offered her tea and biscuits. Was Colin Beswick in the ANC? No. Did she know the where-abouts of Henry, Slovo, Marks, or Dunningham? No. She said she didn't know them; it was Zeke who knew them. They moved her to Pretoria Central, where she was strip-searched by male officers. Naked in a stone room. They said she could end it right then, just give them some names. Nellie refused. She was given a threadbare blanket and a thin mattress that smelled of insecticide, and she shared a cold cell with five other women—two, the oldest, slept on beds, while Nellie and the others slept on the floor. Two days later, Baylor was back with the same questions. No mention of charges; no visitors. No one knew where she was. He came back every few days. Others were talking, he said. I don't know any-thing, she told him.

Four weeks later, a police constable she'd never met was waiting for her in the interrogation room. He was older, an Afrikaner. He didn't take off his cap. Your son, Simon, was killed in a shooting in Alexandra. Nellie's heart exploded, and she cried out in pain. But still she didn't talk. Not that she knew much. Just a name or two. Hazel, Tobias, Tshabalala.

Enough to lead them to Henry and Zeke, maybe even Slovo and some others. But she told them nothing.

Nights were hardest—full of time, dark alone time, full of other women's moans and screams, human peals that bounced off the stone walls, sharp and mad and invisible in the dim prison gloom. Her heart was filled with thoughts of her son, her mind dismayed—why was she alive and he was not, and how could she endure this without him? Moonlight slid across the cement floor. He'd planned to be a teacher or a lawyer like Nelson and Henry. He was so clever, such a good boy. *Thula thula, thula baba.* It seemed like yesterday she was singing lullabies to him. She sang quietly with the women in her cell. *Ukuthula kulo mhlaba wezono.* Peace in this world of sin.

The English-speaking officer, Baylor, visited again, but he seemed tired of his questions, tired of her. Sometimes other police officers stopped at the cell. They just watched, looking through the bars, like cats. After twelve weeks, Nellie was released. There were no charges. She took Thandi and went to live with her parents in Breyton.

THE TREETOPS were silvery; insects screeched. A few tufty clouds swirled in the moonlit sky. Surrounded by sky and stars and endless *veld,* they lay in the living room, stretched and curled on the old leather furniture.

"They wrote letters," Ndolo said. "But she wouldn't show them to us, and after she passed we never found any."

"A remarkable woman," Saul said. He was thinking of his grandmother as well. Six long weeks in prison, not knowing how long she'd be detained.

"Yes. And still found time to nag us about schoolwork," Lillian said.

Ndolo chuckled. "And provocative clothes. She hated us wearing short skirts."

"I wish I could have met her," Saul said.

"Yes." The sisters nodded in unison.

"She would have liked that," Ndolo added.

Saul was trying to tell himself he was cool with Henry's infidelity, with the secrets and their aftermath; it was a difficult time, a crazy time, they were all young and under a lot of pressure. But even as he assured himself it was all okay, or at least excusable, there was a feeling he couldn't suppress. Henry's secret was bigger than Saul's biggest secret, whatever it was, by a mile, exponentially bigger, and as a result Saul felt suddenly discombobulated, like a newborn, mewling and confused, a stranger on earth. How long had it gone on? Did Grams ever find out? Did she know Nellie? She must have. How had it ended? Had he just abandoned Nellie, or had she been the one to walk out? So much that he didn't know, and for a moment the confusion was replaced by anger at his *umkhulu*, the old liar. But the Mkhatshwas bore him no malice, Nellie obviously loved him, and the damage he'd done was mitigated by the lives he'd saved—his own, Glenn's. As for lying to Saul, well, he was undoing that too. This trip was his way of coming clean.

Vusi had succeeded in reconnecting the antenna to the stereo, and now a Kwaito song belted from the living-room speakers. Saul sat tapping his foot, thinking about Nellie, about the unsung heroes who had died for a cause, or whose loved ones had died, or whose lives got ripped apart, who made sacrifices so people they loved could go free, so that a whole country could be free. Not all heroes were so heroic. Gramps had devastated other people's lives—his lover's, his wife's, his son's—forced them to make impossible choices, maybe even got Simon killed. History loves heroes, he thought, but you don't always know who the real heroes are. Saul had known for a while that something was fundamentally wrong with his idea for a documentary, though he couldn't put his finger on it. Now he knew what it was: you can't make a documentary about people who are hidden from history. You need footage, actual images of their lives.

After a while, he excused himself and found his way to the study. He sat at Dunningham's desk and picked up the phone. From the living room came the hum of conversation, a ripple of laughter.

"Dad, hi."

"Saul. Everything okay?" Afternoon at his father's office. He could hear phones ringing, voices in the background.

"Yeah, I just wanted to say hello."

"Where are you?"

"At the Dunninghams' farm, near Kruger Park."

"You okay?"

"Yeah, well, there was a bit of trouble, I almost got robbed, but I'm fine."

"You what?" Glenn's voice rose in panic.

"No big deal. Honest." He shouldn't have said anything; he didn't want his parents to worry. The danger was over now. There was something else he wanted to tell his dad—oh yeah, that he loved him. But he didn't know how to say it. "Don't tell Mom, okay. She'll only worry."

"Okay. Need me to phone Dick, do anything?"

"No, I spoke to him already."

"You sure you're okay?"

"I'm fine, really. I just wanted to call, you know, hear your voice."

"I'm so glad you did. Saulie, what happened? What do you mean, you almost got robbed?

"Grampa had an affair."

Muffled office sounds at the other end of the line.

"I know."

"You never told me."

"I thought about it. But every time I did I decided to let sleeping dogs lie. I figured if he wanted to tell you, he could."

"Gramps must have known that I'd find out."

"He knows you're a smart kid. Anyway, now you know."

"Now I know." He felt a sudden urge to hug his dad. Tears welled in his eyes, and he swatted them away. On the desk in front of him sat a row of framed photos bathed in the yellow glow of the desk lamp—the Dunninghams, various children and grandchildren, he presumed—happy family faces. He thought, you don't change history if that's not what you set out to do, he thought. Maybe you raise a family instead, give your son a home, an education, or shepherd your daughter to safety, not yank them out of their lives and separate them from their mothers when they're kids. Maybe that's a quiet kind of courage too.

"Hey, Dad, I'll try to smuggle some biltong back for you."

"That'd be great, Saul."

"Dad. I love you."

"I love you too, Saulie. Take care of yourself. Be safe, okay?"

"I will."

Saul waited in the study before going back to join the others.

Back in the living room, Vusi had found a bottle of brandy, and Saul poured them each a glass.

He sat quietly for a while, and then softly said, "People like Nellie carried the revolution on their shoulders, you know. And bore the wounds." He was drunk and full of poetry. He raised his glass. "*Ooogy wawa*," he said, and they chuckled and lifted their glasses. "To Nellie."

"To Nellie."

"And Henry," Ndolo said.

"And Henry."

They raised their glasses again, and drank.

V<small>USI</small> <small>FELL</small> asleep in his chair, his mouth open, the brandy snifter on the armrest. The women woke him after a while and prodded him upstairs.

Saul and Londiwe were the last ones awake. They sat on the verandah under a sky phosphorescent with stars, and sipped rooibos tea and gazed out into the night at the moonlit marula and bushwillow trees etched on the horizon.

Did anything happen? Did they kiss, make love passionately in the middle of the *veld*, with the sound of the wind and roaming impala in the distance? No, nothing like that. They said good night and tiptoed upstairs. Alone in his room, Saul masturbated quietly, imagining Londiwe naked in bed with him, straddling him. He fell asleep listening to the muted psalmody of night.

35. Empire State

They ate more cheeseburgers, rode in Checker cabs, walked the busy streets of New York. Dunningham spent his mornings at the Metropolitan Museum and afternoons with Joe Borgese and his friends. Henry and Glenn went to the top of the Empire State Building, saw the Statue of Liberty, shopped at Macy's, bought a Yankees T-shirt for Glenn, a mug and guidebook for Sarah. Glenn was assembling a box of presents for her, a treasure chest for his missing mother. In the evenings, the three of them went to a movie or sat in the hotel room listening to Henry's cassettes, watching TV, or playing cards. Their favourite, though, was charades. Glenn frowned, then signaled film, two words, and acted it out, shooting, riding his steed, shouting silent orders to invisible troops. Henry knew the answer, but it wasn't his turn. They watched the boy take aim, shoot, gallop his horse, swagger like John Wayne across the room—from the door past the beds to the single armchair where Dunningham sat, feigning puzzlement. A moment later: "Of course. *The Alamo.*" Glenn shook hands with Dunningham, hugged his father. The three of them laughing, breaking into song: "Davy, Davy Crockett, king of the wild frontier."

Glenn was alternately enthralled and anxious. Wide-eyed as they drove down the FDR Drive alongside the East River and Welfare Island. But also fretful, distracted, prone to spells of immobility—on his bed, in a chair, in the bathroom. They worried Henry, these episodes, a sudden solitary stillness, as if he had fallen asleep with his eyes open. Then, one day, the questions bubbled out. They were eating breakfast at their favourite diner on Lex.

"Why was Mommy arrested?"

"They just did it to scare her."

"They didn't house arrest her, like you?"

"No. She's in jail because they found some book or magazine. Can you imagine that? In America you can read whatever you like. But she's fine, I promise. Nana and Grampa have been to visit her, our friends too. They'll let her out soon."

"When?"

"At most, in about eighty more days. Probably less."

"And then she'll come here?"

"Yes."

He stared dejectedly at his plate of pancakes. "I'll be ten by then. She'll miss my birthday."

A few days later, Henry went down to the lobby to buy a newspaper before breakfast. He was about to enter the newsagent's kiosk when he heard a familiar accent. A South African man in a grey suit was asking the concierge how much a double room cost and whether his friends had checked in yet. Henry had used a fake name when he'd registered, and as far as he could tell, the young concierge didn't volunteer the names of any guests.

Still, he was spooked. Back in the room, he waited for Glenn to go to the bathroom before speaking to Dick.

"You don't know he was looking for one of us," Dunningham said.

"No, but he may have been."

"Could you really hear them properly, though? Are you sure he wasn't Dutch or Australian? Hen, aren't you being a bit paranoid?"

"Maybe."

"No reciprocity for political crimes. They can't arrest us. What're they going to do, shoot us?"

"Maybe we should move. We can't stay in this hotel forever."

"Well, I suppose that's true," Dunningham conceded.

They left later that morning. Took a taxi to the Blakely Hotel. Glenn was tired, cranky. He didn't want the tiny bit of routine, the shred of home he'd established, to be taken from him. He was even less happy when, two days later, they packed up again and ferried their suitcases, an electric kettle, and three bags of groceries to a one-bedroom apartment on Sullivan Street, which Joe Borgese had arranged for them. To lift Glenn's spirits, Henry suggested a matinee, and so they all went off to see *The Great Escape*. Afterwards they walked through Washington Square and listened to the folk singers and looked at the buildings and imagined what each one would look like if it were a skyscraper, stretched three, four, ten times taller, soaring into the sky. They cooked Chef Boy-Ar-Dee ravioli in the little galley kitchen, and Dunningham and Henry drank red wine.

THE NEXT day they bought posters to brighten the little apartment—a Formula One racing car and a large black-and-white photograph of the Empire State Building rising from the city streets, massive and majestic. After they'd pinned them to the walls, they sat on the couch in the narrow living room, admiring their handiwork and sipping root beer in front of the window fan.

"Are we going to go home?" the boy asked.

"We are home." Henry didn't know what else to say. Nothing that was true would comfort the boy.

DUNNINGHAM ANNOUNCED that he would be returning to London in a couple of days. Daisy was waiting for him. That night they went to *Breakfast at Tiffany's*, even though it wasn't really appropriate for a nine-year-old. When the three of them walked out into the hot evening on West Eighth Street, Henry realised that each of them was in love with Audrey Hepburn, and each was missing a distant woman—mother, lover, wife.

"CAN WE get a dog when Mom comes?"

"Yes, good idea. We'll get a dog."

"Can we go and visit her if she doesn't come soon?"

"No, we can't go and visit. We'll have to wait. We can buy nice things for her."

"I miss Janey."

"I know. I miss her too."

"Is she in jail with Mommy? Or did she go home?"

"She's at her house, I think. Or with friends. Not with Mommy."

"Don't you even know?"

"No, I'm afraid I don't. But I'm sure Mommy knows."

"Why don't you care about anyone?"

"Why would you say that, Glenn?"

"Because."

"I do care, of course I do. I care about you. I love you. More than anything."

"You don't. You don't keep your promises. You say things, but you don't mean them. You just leave people behind."

He tried to hug him, but the boy drew back and pushed his palms against Henry's chest, not punching, just pressing, as if something inside Henry were expanding and had to be contained.

"Leaving you and Mommy, that was the most difficult thing I've ever done. I didn't want to. You must know that. And I do keep my promises. I, we, we've had to make some very difficult choices. This is not what we wanted, me and Mommy. I had to leave home. It was either that or spend a long time in jail."

The pushing had stopped now. Glenn's arms hung at his sides.

"Because you want black people to be free."

"Because I want all people to be free."

"Can we write to Janey and then she can write to us?"

"That's a great idea. We'll find out her address and send her a letter, maybe even send her a present from New York. She'd like that."

Even as he said it, he knew they wouldn't do it. They wouldn't find her address, and if they did he wouldn't mail the letter. He didn't know how postage stamps and post office codes worked. It didn't matter, anyway. It was too big a risk to take. And so he knew that he would lie to his son again, even though he was loath to do it. What other option was there?

"It's not fair." Glenn's face crumpled. "Nobody said that . . . I just want to see them. Mommy and Janey and my friends and everybody."

Henry wrapped his arms around Glenn and the boy allowed himself to be hugged now, and they breathed in, breathed out together, not moving, just breathing together on the brown couch.

"I would do anything for you, Glenn. Anything. I never ever want to lie to you or break a promise. Okay?"

"Okay."

A small sound, almost a whimper, as Glenn shuddered and his chest thrust forward and then relaxed again, and Henry held him, the boy's hot, tear-streaked face on his neck. He felt they were floating, he and Glenn, weightless yet also heavy, as if the space between them and the ceiling were pushing down on them, leaden air, compressing and also bearing them up.

DICK'S LAST night, they went with Joe Borgese to an Italian restaurant on MacDougal Street and then to Gerde's. "Don't let the kid get drunk," the guy at the door mumbled as they entered the bar. The bartender poured Glenn a root beer in a pint glass and Dick and Henry and Joe drank beer. A little later Blind Boy Grunt took the stage, a harmonica around his neck.

"That's Bob Dylan," Borgese said, leaning in.

"Where?"

"On stage."

"I thought that was Blind Boy something or other?" Dick asked.

"Same guy."

"Bloody marvellous. Bob Dylan. Hen, you hear that?"

On stage, the scrawny guy in jeans and suede boots began strumming his guitar and blowing his harmonica, kicking the back of his right boot to the beat. "Don't the clouds look lonesome shining across the sea." When he finished the song, he waved to Glenn and Glenn waved back, and Henry ordered him another root beer and ruffled his hair.

Walking home along Bleecker Street, Henry told Glenn the story of his Great-Uncle Zalman who'd sailed on his cello down a river in Latvia, to freedom.

"Will John Glenn orbit the earth again?"

"I don't know. I'm sure there'll be another mission. We'll go to the library and find out."

"Does Mommy miss me?"

"Of course she does. You're her big boy. She loves you and wishes she was with us right now."

"Where is she? Where is the prison? What's it called?"

"Johannesburg. It's called the Old Fort."

"Will she bring my things? I want my models and my soldiers and my Batman comics and my soccer jersey."

"She'll bring some of them."

"This lady's flat smells funny."

FUNDS WERE running low. The wad of banknotes Dunningham had pressed on him would last another month or two, maybe three if they scrimped and saved. Henry spoke to Bob Gornick, who arranged some meetings with law firms. One of the lawyers he met suggested he interview at IBM. It was time to give Glenn a proper home, and Henry liked the idea of moving out to the suburbs. They'd set up a house, get Glenn into school, and when Sarah arrived everything would be ready. She'd fit in, like the missing piece of a jigsaw puzzle. They'd go to the beach, visit Florida or California. They'd have their things shipped from Johannesburg, and then it would really feel like home. They'd have another baby. It was Gornick who suggested that Henry speak to a dean at Stony Brook University.

36. Long Distance

Glenn ran. Legs pumping, propelling himself across Washington Square, zigzagging around pedestrians, parked cars, the silver hedgehog buses. He was quick and nimble, and it felt good to run. It would feel good to curl beside his mother, to feel her and smell her. He'd been stashing quarters and dimes when he bought Hershey's Bars and Spiderman comics. He ran past the swings and sandpit, didn't look back: he knew he'd put a lot of distance between himself and his father. He was invisible now, lost in the crowd. He knew what time it was in South Africa, knew exactly what he would say.

He fed his coins into the phone with trembling hands, and some of them fell, tinkling and blinking on the sidewalk. He spoke to an operator, fed more coins. Another operator, a sound like waves crashing.

The phone rang and rang. It was the only sound he heard, the double peal an echo of itself. Patches of sunlight pooled around his feet on the steel floor of the phone booth. The ringing engulfed him, and he waited, listening, staring at his shoes. Finally someone answered. Then he had to wait again, a minute, another minute. He fed more slippery coins and pictured phone cables five fathoms under the sea, fish, and pirate galleons.

"I'm sorry, we cannot connect outside calls to detainees. You must phone and arrange a visit."

He let the receiver drop, then returned it to its silver cradle. When he turned around, there was his dad, a few feet away, waiting.

He ran into his father's arms and let himself be smothered and held and lifted.

"I just wanted to speak to Mommy."

"I know. We'll phone her. As soon as we can. I promise."

SHE CRAVED solitude and quiet. Lay in bed and listened to the radio, windows shut, curtains closed, gazing at the ceiling. She had never noticed all the life up there, forms and shapes hiding in the paint. A snowflake splotch; a camel; a girl bending over; the circle of light that rose above the lamp, shadows dimpling the curtain. She didn't sleep much, didn't bathe, ate very little—oranges, canned soup, chocolate, and biscuits. She could smell her animal self, a vinegary, unfamiliar, oddly male odour. In prison she'd been too cold to sweat. Prison smelled of bleach and piss and time. Each night a lonely desert.

There were fish that lived at the bottom of the ocean. She'd read about them with Glenn, in one of his schoolbooks. Nearly blind, gelatinous and ugly, they didn't need much oxygen and were impervious to the pressure on the ocean floor. They craved the cold and wanted only to be left alone. She felt like one of those deep-sea fish—content and slow, unaccompanied.

She didn't want prison to change her, but it had. Eight days of freedom, and she'd barely been outdoors, had seen only a handful of people—her parents twice, brave Hilda, a few men and women who had been in prison themselves. She liked speaking on the telephone, rang her mother once or twice a day. She knew the phone might be tapped, so they spoke about the weather, how she was feeling, what she was eating. Her mother listened to a radio serial, and gave Sarah regular updates on the daily drama of the characters' lives.

She wanted Sarah to see a doctor, and Sarah promised but didn't make an appointment. She didn't want another interrogation. She hadn't been sleeping well, but it didn't matter; she didn't mind being awake, lying in her own bed, safe until tomorrow. Some of the women had sung quiet hymns after lights out. "Nearer, my God, to thee" and "Silent Night." Timorous voices bouncing off the bricks. In due course she'd bring Janey and Ndimande back and get things back to normal. But not today. She liked her deep-sea bedroom, lying quite still in her bed, ensconced in bedclothes and dim light—mollusced and warm. The sun and shifting sky, the city and its people kept outside, beyond, at bay.

The phone startled her. Then again, just about anything startled her these days—a dog barking, a car door, a rake scraping. Eleven days now—or was it twelve?—eating without appetite, tired but unable to sleep.

"Hello." Even her own voice surprised her now—loud, crackly.

"Darling." Henry's voice, the voice that used to sound like home. Used to.

Hazel had arranged the call, a safe telephone in a safe house; someone had phoned Henry with the number, and here he was, the familiar voice, only thinner, piped in from halfway around the world, wrapped in whooshing waves.

"Henry."

She'd waited half the day for the call, sitting in a stranger's house, surrounded by old rugs and polished period furniture. A trio of blue bowls on the top shelf of the bookcase, some lilies in a chipped vase, splayed and drooping. In prison there were no flowers, only a bar-crossed view of red rooftops and sky.

"How are you? Are you all right? I've been so worried." Though distorted by the long-distance cables, his voice sounded bright and enthusiastic. She pictured him in a carpeted room filled with modern American furniture, a busy Manhattan street outside. She imagined a large television set and, for some reason, a canary-yellow washing machine.

"I'm okay."

"Sarah, I'm so sorry."

"I'm all right now. I'm fine."

"Good. That's good. When are you coming?"

"Henry, I can't."

"Because of prison?"

"I just can't. Not right now."

"I'll take care of everything. Just get on the plane. You'll see. It was your idea, New York."

"None of this was my idea. You know that. Just send Glenn. Take him on a nice holiday, somewhere fun, then send him home." She'd sat all morning, drinking tea and working out the best way—how to make it easiest for Glenn.

Henry said nothing for a while, and then, "I can't send him back. Sarah, my darling, we talked about this. Things are getting worse there. We decided. We don't want Glenn to make his future there."

He sounded so certain. Hunky dory, *jolly soos 'n lolly*. She looked over at the wilting lilies on the mahogany tea table.

"I'm not talking about the future," she said, leaning forward on the narrow settee. "I'm talking about right now." She hadn't expected outright refusal, hadn't expected an argument at all.

"I can't send him back there only to bring him here again. I won't. That's not fair or sensible."

A pause. If they'd been in the same room, he'd have given her that look now, his head tilted to the side, suggesting assent even when there was none.

"If you come here and you don't like it and you want to take him back, then we'll put it to him and he can decide. But I'm not going back to face certain arrest. Glenn's happy. You'll see. And you'll like it here. I know you will. Come to America. Come to your family."

After she hung up, she banged the phone against her forehead and received its numbing, drumming pain. She drove to the shops on the way home, bought tea, fruit, milk, and canned soups, devoured a chocolate bar in the parking lot before driving home.

She opened the curtains and windows a few days later and stood shivering, looking out at her unfamiliar garden. Closed the curtains again, burrowed back into bed. The next day she ran a bath, luxuriated in lavender-scented bubbles, washed her hair and cupped bubbles in her palms, blowing them onto the tiles, watching them clot and creep down to the frothy water. She sat on the floor in Glenn's room, picked up a model plane, turned it over as she examined it, ran her hands across his school blazer, pressed his pyjamas and shirts to her face and inhaled hungrily.

Maybe Henry was right. Maybe she needed to force herself to go, to leave—one foot in front of the other, onto the plane, out of the country. Funny, in prison she'd felt so sure of the future; it was something real, visible every time she closed her eyes. Now she wasn't so sure.

Tea with Hilda. Esmé Goldberg had left for England with her children; Hilda thought it the right thing to do. She had taken Patrick, just fifteen, to visit Rusty in prison. The sight of his father, thin and drawn, surrounded by bars and guards, had shocked the boy, and he'd barely managed to say a word. Sarah felt grateful that Glenn had been spared this fate.

She was part of him, her boy, and he was part of her. Her missing limb, her missing love. But even the sound of his voice was beginning to fade. She wanted him back, but not now, not yet. Maybe after Ndimande and Janey returned, after the house was a proper house again. Maybe when she was cooking and entertaining and playing the piano again, when the nightmares stopped and she was ready for sunlight.

THEY SPENT a day on Park Avenue, toured the Pan Am Building and the Seagram Building, rode the elevator to the eighteenth floor of Lever House. One especially hot day, he and his dad took a train to Long Beach Island, where they swam in the sea and examined the houses built on stilts. At first he was cross that the shops didn't sell *koeksisters*, but he settled for an ice cream, and they sat together on the hot beach, licking sticky droplets from their fingers.

They built model planes together and watched television in the middle of the day. *My Three Sons* and *Bonanza*. Most evenings they walked in Washington Square, then came home and cooked supper. He liked his Chef Boy-Ar-Dee spaghetti piled high with Parmesan cheese on top. They laid the table with paper napkins and the cracked plates they found in the kitchen cupboard. Home. Not home.

37. A Leaf at the Edge of the Sky

The wind howls, rattling the windows, bullying the last leaves off their branches. He is in his armchair, slippered feet warm and heavy on the carpet. How long has he been sitting here? He doesn't know. The sky is like an upside-down porcelain bowl, blue-glazed, resting on the tops of buildings and water towers and the bare oak tree across the street. He likes the fading light at the end of the day. He remembers a different chair in a different living room, Holly cooking in the kitchen, the radio on NPR. Or Sarah, a long time ago, him with a scotch and the newspaper, she with a book, a glass of sherry perhaps, the radio playing, or an LP record. A car honks. Steam floats up from the building across the street. The oak tree is resolute—knobbly, arthritic. Here and there, a tenacious leaf clings to the end of a branch at the edge of the dim blue sky. Sometimes Sarah would play the piano—Bach or Schumann—while Janey gave Glenn his bath. They'd lied to her, the doctors, at the end, just as his own doctors were probably lying to him now.

HE STILL walks most days, not to the park, but along Van Brunt and up King Street to the waterfront, a mess of rubble and abandoned stuff—wire hangers, shoes, broken glass, plastic bottles, smashed TVs, hubcaps, charred wood. In the river, plastic bags and mucky branches tangle and bob against the embankment. Beyond the murk, the water flows cleanly, a real river, swift and determined.

A splash of whiskey in his tea in the afternoon. The milk is three days past its expiry date but it smells okay. A nip when the sun goes down, with the television on, a glass of whiskey or cheap red wine mixed with a bit of port. Warms the heart. His eyes are crap. When he peers into the fridge he has to wait for the shapes to settle into things he recognises—milk, can of beans, yoghurt. Driving in a taxi, the world flows and ebbs, things mash and unmash, warble in and out of focus in dizzying colours. Henry, gripping the armrest, presses himself back into the seat like a frightened child as cars, lampposts, and pedestrians swim past.

He's been to the house in Annandale. Went there for Thanksgiving and Christmas day. Sometimes goes for Sunday lunch. It's big and clean and feels half empty. Is Glenn happy? He's never known when Glenn is happy. After Dunningham left, they were alone together in the Sullivan Street apartment. He bought coloured markers and paint and paper and they covered the walls with pictures of cars, buildings, grids, and swirls of primary colours. He told Glenn he didn't know when they'd move to a proper house, or when Mommy would arrive.

Glenn never did get his mother back, nor did he get a second mother. Well, there was Melanie, who moved in with them in the first house in Stony Brook. But the thing with Melanie eroded, then ended abruptly. There was Anne, a divorcée, two kids, both a bit younger than Glenn. They'd go to the beach together, have cookouts with the kids at each others' houses, but they never moved in together. What had happened? She'd moved somewhere. Seattle or California. And

Sarah? She had served her time, and the police kept her passport for a while, but after her release they left her alone. She was introduced to Peter Hirsch at a cocktail party. She'd sent photos of little Alison and Brett, her cute blond babies.

S OMETIMES HIS sight goes gauzy. It's as if a curtain descends across his eyes. The thinnest cotton, but somehow also liquid, leaky. Quick and slippery, it happens without warning. The world wobbles, shapes melt. Sometimes, in dreams, she calls to him. Sarah. She waves, or sits with her hands together as if in prayer, looking up at him. *Kom, Henry.*

O R HIS father with the *tefillin* and leather-bound *mahzor* he'd brought all the way from Lithuania. *Baruch Shem Kavod Malchuto L'Olam Vaed.* There's the little synagogue, too, on Hereford Road and also the priest at his school in Port Elizabeth, Father Slayton. He can't remember what happened yesterday, but he remembers the synagogue, the dark pews, the brass lights, the old school priest. *Wherefore have ye beguiled us, saying, We are very far from you; when ye dwell among us?* Sometimes Nellie appears, in a wet-grass garden. When he saw her again thirty years had passed. They were both old. She wasn't loved enough or thanked enough or mourned enough, not by him, anyway. For years after he came to America, he'd made mental notes of things to tell her, share with her. Harlem, Coltrane, Kennedy, Wes Montgomery. She'd been his sanctuary and his saviour, his fugitive love, and he's never stopped missing her.

G LENN VISITS every two or three weeks. Sometimes they meet at the Oyster Bar in Grand Central Station or the delicatessen one level down—pastrami sandwiches or beef hot dogs with all the trimmings. When he tells his son he isn't feeling a hundred percent or when Glenn goes to see a client in Brooklyn, he takes a taxi to Red Hook, brings sandwiches or soggy hotdogs and unpacks the bag of groceries that Holly has sent. Saul lives in the East Village now. He's working for an Internet startup, thinking about law school, thinking about travelling. His girlfriend's name is Sabrina; her parents were born in Vietnam. *Uitlanders. Fremder mensch.* Saul brings her to visit occasionally and they walk to The Good Fork on Van Brunt. Mostly he comes alone, though, once a fortnight or so. It'd be nice to see the boy more often. Joe Borgese lives in Florida now. They have lunch or dinner when he comes to visit his daughter. Good old Joe.

S<small>AUL COMES</small> to Red Hook the most, sometimes just for a few minutes, a cup of tea, a game of backgammon. It was Saul who found him shivering and weak, took one look at him and bundled him into a car. By then he was malnourished and dehydrated, seeing things that weren't there—a horse on Flatbush Avenue, soldiers in the hospital elevator. Five hours later, he had surgery. A kidney abscess. Jamaican nurses in floral scrubs called him handsome. Such a gentleman, they said. Names and numbers swirled on a dry erase board across from the foot of the bed. He shared a room with a man who was going to have a gangrenous leg amputated. The first days in the hospital his mind played tricks. Acute dementia, they called it. Couldn't remember the name of the president, or who had just left the room. Then they said it was delirium, caused by the anaesthesia and the dehydration that had pre-ceded it, and it would pass. Delirium moon. Baboon. But his health returned and his mind got itself back to normal. New normal. Glenn came down, settled him at home, set up an emergency contact, a private nurse he could phone night or day. Holly came the following week. Sometimes he puts salt in his coffee. He eats tinned beans, pasta, and tomato sauce, not Chef Boy-Ar-Dee anymore. Once in a while he forgets to buy groceries, or eat. But most days he's fine.

THE MONEY'S drying up. Glenn took everything they got from the house. That's okay, there's still the rent from the downstairs tenant, his retirement checks, and modest dividends, but he has to pay the mortgage, doctors, cleaning lady. He lies to Glenn. Tells him he has enough, tells him not to worry. It's all right. Not broke yet. A little something to leave Glenn and Holly and Saul and Nellie's family in his will. Not as much as he'd have liked, but it probably never is. Something better than nothing. Love better than death. Sometimes he rides the bus to Seventh Avenue and walks in Prospect Park. Careful as he crosses the stream of people on bicycles, skateboards, Rollerblades. He hates Rollerblades. Can't abide boom boxes either, or drumming circles. He takes the train to Stony Brook occasionally, for law school parties or dinner at a colleague's house. He travelled to London for Rusty's funeral. Hilda moved back to South Africa, to Sea Point, to live near her son. That's where she died, three years ago—or was it longer? *We have the whole world to be free in.*

HE LOVES the pale, breathless sky as the light fades, the steely smell of night. Sometimes he thinks he's back in the house in Observatory, under an African sky. He remembers the flat on Cliff Street. Port Elizabeth was unimaginably bright and empty. Light in the alleys and on the streets, sun on the water, bouncing off the dark shiny backs of automobiles, sun in the trees and on the grass that grew everywhere, even in the middle of the city. Herschel Rabinowitz drove a Hudson. He likes this armchair, this apartment, the expansive sky. The rug that doesn't fit lies rolled up in the study like a big log. He doesn't want to move to a retirement home. No, sir. Fuck that shit. He likes the noble oak tree across the road, its boughs taller than the streetlights and telephone wires. What's for supper, Janey? The window mullions are painted white, and it is through these frames that he beholds the world—the big oak tree, the sky that comforts him. Sunset paints the walls pink, the awnings and windows across the road, frayed clouds, white stars at night. *Wayse shtern.*

SOMETIMES HE forgets, and thinks he is in Africa. His eyes play tricks and he sees the land, arid and beautiful. Leaves and branches bending in the breeze, thorn tree shadows on the *veld*. He loves the trees and sky. And he is glad that he lived there.

IT'S SNOWING again. A fine white powder settling on the roof-tops, clinging to the branches. Better not to walk today. The streets may be icy. Sometimes there are kids at the end of the block. They watch him like wolves. What do they see? A funny old man? Possible prey? Better to stay home. A splash of whiskey in his rooibos, doesn't need milk tonight, see what's on television. Better to stay put.

ACKNOWLEDGMENTS

Huge heartfelt thanks to:

Martin Shepard, Judith Shepard, and Alison Lowry, for believing.
The wonderful team at The Permanent Press.

Experts and enablers, muses and mentors:
Gertrude Maseko; Ndolo Mekwa; Makaziwe Ramateng; Pier and Philip Myburgh; Toni Strasburg; Amanda Davis; Eve Mothibe; Lila Cecil; Mthandeni Khumalo; Nadine Gordimer; Peter Carey; the gang at Mass Transmit.

The MacDowell Colony, where this book was born.

Consiglieri and readers who provided invaluable guidance:
Jennifer Robinson, Julie Barer, Adrienne Brodeur, Lisa Selin Davis, Juliet Koss, Susan Golomb, and Jean Fryer.

My family, who helped directly and indirectly:
June and David Schneider; John, Jack, Harry, and Sophie Schneider; Hope Cohn; Jessica, Tessa, Jonathan, Mark, and Claire Katzenellenbogen; Doda, Sara, Julia, and Frances Levy; Peter Saville; Max Henry Levy Schneider.

Of many insightful and valuable books I read, I am especially indebted to:
The World That Was Ours by Hilda Bernstein; *Rivonia's Children* by Glenn Frankel; *Side by Side* by Helen Joseph; *Long Walk to Freedom* by Nelson Mandela; *The Road to Democracy*

in South Africa by South African Democracy Education Trust; *The Young Mandela* by David James Smith.

It is my hope that this book pays tribute to the many heroes—both sung and unsung—of South Africa's Struggle and liberation. They moved a mountain.